THE UNCOVERED DREAM

Diane Ziomek

The Uncovered Dream
Copyright 2014 by Diane Ziomek
ISBN: 978-0-9877811-7-8
eISBN: 978-0-9877811-8-5

Independently Published by
Diane Ziomek
Box 383
Mannville, AB T0B 2W0
http://www.dianeziomek.ca

Warning: There is some mature content within the pages of this book; please use your discretion.

Cover photo provided by A to Z Alpacas and is copyrighted
www.atozalpacas.com

For

My loyal readers. Without you my writing would be pointless.

Things aren't always as they seem.

CHAPTER ONE

January was a new month and the beginning of a new year. Sam had met the man she had only dreamed about (although her dreams never had him owning a hardware store) and she was fitting into the community. It was the same community that had spent years hiding the existence of her new home and all it stood for. Plus, it was the very community that would help her piece together her past.

Fate takes twists and turns, and Sam was about to learn more about it (whether she wanted to or not). As she was getting ready to go into town one morning, she heard a knock at the door. She opened it to find an officer standing there with an envelope in his hand.

"Samantha Jones?" he asked.
"Yes, I'm Sam," she replied.
"I'm Officer Barnes. Sorry to bother you but I have an order to serve you with this subpoena.
"A subpoena? For what?!"
"The paperwork has all the details Ma'am; I have simply been instructed to make sure you received them. Could you sign here please?" and handed her a pen and a clipboard with a sheet of paper attached to it. She quickly scanned the sheet and signed on the line he pointed to. It was to confirm she had been given the documents, and that the officer was in no way responsible for any material contained within.
"Thank you Ms. Jones," he said as she handed him back the

clipboard and pen "I do hope your day gets better."

As Sam closed the door, she opened the envelope. She read the subpoena and couldn't believe what she was seeing. Her mother was suing her! What in the world was she expecting to gain?

She set the papers on the counter and let Bear out into the backyard. She was going to take him along, but decided today was not a good day after all. She now had extra stops to make, and she wasn't sure just how long she would be. It was best if he was left at home.

While Bear played in the snow, Sam made her grocery list. She didn't feel much like shopping now, but knew it was best if she did. Joe had told her the day before there was a blizzard on the way, and she wanted to be prepared. She didn't want to be snowed in without a good supply of food, water and other necessities. It could be days before she was able to leave the yard.

Bear barked and she let him in, and he went straight into his kennel. He was accustomed to the routine now, and there were days she didn't even close the kennel door. Since she was going to be gone for several hours, she closed it. She was still uneasy about him having run of the house while she was gone. She had watched "Turner and Hooch", and although he wasn't the same breed of dog, he could do just as much damage.

Sam gathered her purse, cell phone and paperwork and got into her truck. Her first stop was going to be Joe's so she turned left as she pulled out of her drive. She could feel a headache creeping in; something she frequently got whenever her mother entered the picture. She knew then it was going to be a very long day.

When she turned into Joe's drive she almost ran into the police cruiser as it was leaving. Officer Barnes was making his rounds it seemed. She mouthed an "I'm sorry" and let him pass before she went any further. He smiled and waved apologetically as he went by, and she wondered who else he was delivering paperwork to.

Sam parked her truck next to Joe's and went to the door. She gave a quick knock followed by "Dad?" as she opened the door.

"Good morning Sam! What brings you by so early?" He was much too cheerful for someone who had just had a visit from a police officer.

Sam showed him the envelope, and he responded with "I see you had an early morning visitor as well."

"Yup! What joy did he bring you?"

"Divorce papers. And you?"

"She is suing me for hardship, of all things. I didn't think such a thing even existed!"

Joe could feel the anger rising within. It was one thing for Sally to divorce him, but to expect Sam to give her the inheritance was ludicrous! How could she expect such a thing when he was the one who financially supported her all these years, even after Sam was on her own?

"Well Sam, it looks like we both need a lawyer - and I know just the man for the job." With that, he proceeded to call Keith and explained what they were faced with.

After he hung up the phone Joe looked at her and said "We have some homework to do. Keith said we should be as prepared as possible - which means going back to even before my accident. I don't remember much of that Sam."

Sam's heart was breaking. She could see in Joe's eyes he was very afraid of the outcome if he couldn't remember. If only Uncle Chad were still alive. He was the only one who would be able to provide the details they needed. Or maybe, just maybe, Jason and Emily could provide some insight. the question was, would they?

After her visit with Joe, Sam drove to town with her grocery list in hand. It was almost noon, so she went to the hardware store to see Kody. He greeted her with a big smile as she walked through the door.

"Hi Sam! What brings you into town today? You know there's a storm on its way."

"That's one of the reasons I'm here. The other is to see if you've had lunch yet."

Kody's face lit up. "As a matter of fact, I was just on my way out shortly. Would you care to join me?"

"Of course I'll join you, but first I have to check a few things off my list."

"Let me know when you're ready. I have to wait for Sandra to get back anyway. I'll be in the back."

Sam went through her list and picked up candles, wooden matches, a barbecue lighter, extra lighter fluid and a couple of toys for Bear. As she paid for her items she saw Sandra walk through the door. After taking her bags out to her truck she went back inside to let Kody know she was ready.

"Chinese or subs?" he asked as they walked out of the store, hand in hand.

"Chinese sounds good. Besides, it's quieter there and I need to talk to you about something."

Kody didn't like the sound of that, but he tried not to jump to conclusions. He was sure that what she wanted to talk about had nothing to do with him, but it still didn't stop the thought from crossing his mind.

As they waited for their order, Sam took the envelope out of her purse and handed it to Kody. "I was wondering if you could help Dad and me out, since you seem to know a little more of my family history than I do?"

He breathed a sigh of relief when he read the papers she had handed him. He silently chagrined himself to jumping to conclusions. "You can't be serious! She honestly expects you to hand it all over to her?"

"Apparently! I will never understand that woman. I just don't know if I can remember enough to put up a good defense. I'm really hoping my cousins come through on this; I'll give them a call when I get home. They might be ready to talk. I know they weren't happy when they found out the estate was mine, but I know for a fact they won't want her to get any of it. I just hope by now they know the reasoning behind it."

"All you can do is ask Sam. I'm sure they aren't completely heartless. Perhaps you should invite them out so they can see first-hand what their dad helped build. Maybe it's time for a family meeting."

"You're right Kody. It has been awhile since I spent any time with them, and they are family. I think they would like it out there, and there is no shortage of space."

Sam felt a little better knowing the odds were in her favour. She had spent enough time with her cousins to know they weren't horrible people. As she thought about it, she realized the shock of losing their dad was probably still very real. She knew it was time to make amends and work together with them.

"That smells good. Lets' eat!" Sam was brought back to reality with the sound of Kody's voice as the food arrived.

CHAPTER TWO

Sam arrived at home just as the light was beginning to fade. There weren't many hours of daylight this time of year, and she tried to take advantage of them as much as she could. It had been one of those days where she saw a good portion of it through her truck window.

Bear was excited to see her, and she could hear his tail thumping against the side of the kennel. "Just a few more minutes Bear," she said. "I want to bring the groceries in first."

As she unpacked the bags from the grocery and hardware stores, she watched Bear roll around in the snow. He then went from tree to tree and marked his territory. She still couldn't get over how he could pee just a little, stop, walk, then pee some more. It never ceased to amaze her even though she had seen dogs doing it for as long as she could remember.

After she had everything put away, she went through her contact list on her phone and found Jason and Emily's phone numbers. She decided to call Jason first - she expected him to be more cooperative than Emily.

"Hello?" she heard when he picked up the phone.
"Jason? It's Sam. How are you?"
"Sam! So good to hear from you! How have you been?" That was not the reaction she had been expecting.
"I have been okay, thanks! I know I should have called sooner, but I

have been getting reacquainted with Dad. I'm so sorry!"

"It's okay Sam. How is Uncle Joe anyway? I was so glad to hear he's doing better. We haven't seen much of him in the last ten years or so."

"About that...I was wondering if you and Emily would like to come for a visit? Mom has filed for divorce and is suing me for hardship. We would appreciate it if you two could help fill in some of the blanks."

"I can only speak for myself, but I'm sure Emily will agree to come along. It would be great to see you again - and Uncle Joe. I would love a tour of your new place. Oh, and Sam, I owe you an apology. I had a talk with Keith a few weeks ago and he filled me in. Emily knows the reasoning behind it all too; I'm pretty sure she'll be on board."

"Thanks Jason," she said with tears in her eyes. "You have no idea how much better talking to you has made me feel. Do you know how to get here?"

"Not really, but give me a land location and I'll GPS it. I'll take Emily with me - I'll just tell her we're going on a road trip. Let me get some arrangements made and we'll be there in a couple of days."

"Sounds great! Watch the weather before you set out - we're supposed to be getting a storm moving in. I'll text you the land location. It'll be great to see you two again Jason."

After she hung up, Sam called Joe and told him about her conversation with Jason. He sounded relieved that there wouldn't be any problems getting at least Jason on board. He wasn't quite sure about Emily, but time would tell.

Sam looked through her cupboards and pantry to make sure she had enough food for company. She wished she would have made the phone call before she went into town, because she could have bought extra groceries. She had gotten into the habit of buying extra every time she went grocery shopping, just because it was winter and she wanted to be prepared in case of bad weather. She decided she had stockpiled enough, and even with company there would be enough to last over a week.

After double checking on the groceries, she went out to the suite above the garage. She hadn't been out there much since her friends had been out, and wanted to wash the bedding. She also wanted to make sure there were extra pillows, blankets and a few basic necessities available. Her cousins could decide who got the bedroom and who got the sofa. She decided she would make up the guest room in the house as well, in case they preferred to stay there.

By the time evening had arrived, Sam had everything ready for her company. Now, if only the weather cooperated so they could arrive when planned. She had sent Jason a basic set of directions along with the land location, and was quite confident he could easily find it. She knew they weren't going to be there for at least a couple of days, but she wanted everything to be ready. Plus, she felt a little anxiety and wanted to keep busy. There was also the matter of piecing together her past and the weeks Joe lost; she wanted to have as much ready as possible.

Sam spent the following day trying to remember her past, and in chronological order. Her method of making notes for her writing assignments came in handy. She was able to fill in some milestones and events for each year for as far back as she could remember. Her notebook started with the year Sally and Joe were married and continued to the present. She had designated five pages per year; she would fill in the blanks after talking to her dad and cousins.

Along with her notebook, she decided to give one each to her dad, Jason and Emily. (It was at this point she was glad she had taken advantage of the Back-to-School sales at the Staples store in the city.)

In the city, Jason and Emily made arrangements for the staff to take care of business while they were away. (Jason had decided it was best to let his sister know what was going on; she wouldn't appreciate him if he sprung a road trip on her, especially if they were going to be gone a few days.) It was a slow time, as January always was and they had no doubts about the competence of their staff. They didn't usually take time off together, so Jason knew there would be some concerns voiced. He called for a staff meeting to inform everyone of their upcoming absence. The staff was close, even though there were more than twenty members. They had been employees for several years and had come to consider Jason and Emily (and each other) their family. Chad didn't believe in running a business that had a high turnover, so he did what he could to hire the most compatible people. Occasionally someone just didn't "click", but those times were few and far between. They had only had to fire one person in the last ten years.

"Good afternoon everyone," said Jason after he got everyone's attention. "We have called this brief meeting to let you know we will be gone for a few days. We have some family business to take care of out of town and both need to be there."

There was a buzz of questions and whispering, with each employee speculating why they were going to be gone. For such a small number of people, they sure got loud in a hurry.

Jason clapped his hands loudly to get everyone's attention once again. "I understand your concerns, but be rest assured we won't be more than a couple hours away. We don't anticipate being gone for more than a few days this time, and will possibly be gone again in a few weeks. For those of you who are wondering, no one is ill and we are not making any changes. It's quite the opposite actually; we are going to spend some time with our Uncle Joe and his daughter Sam"

Jason could hear sighs of relief when he said there would be no changes. He recalled the upset of the staff when Chad announced his retirement; they did not adapt to change well, especially when it came to the chain of command. As nice as it was to be a close-knit business, Jason wondered if it was perhaps a downfall at the same time.

"Leon (a senior staff member who had earned the respect of all) will be in charge while we are away. Everyone knows their role in the company, so lets keep things running smoothly, shall we? Oh, and go easy on Leon - he's not as young as he used to be." With that, the mood in the room lightened and Leon looked at Jason, rolled his eyes and shook his head.

"Be careful Mr. Jones; you'll be my age one day - and I fully expect to still be here running circles around you."

After the staff filed out of the room, Jason talked to Leon and briefly let him know why they were going to be away. He also went over what needed to be done over the next few days, and together they came up with a game plan.

Back at the estate it was business as usual. Sam finished   her assignments, and Joe spent the time getting the equipment ready in the barn. He was thankful he had something to keep him busy, but it didn't stop the thoughts completely. He knew he was going to have to try hard to remember; his future depended on it. After some thought and an "Ah hah" moment, he called Julie.

"Good afternoon, Julie Smyth speaking. How can I help you?"
"Hi Julie, it's Joe. I was wondering if you had a few minutes?"
"Of course Joe! I always have time for you; what can I do for you?"

Joe had a thought cross his mind, but instead told her about the divorce and hardship lawsuit against Sam. He also asked her if she had any thoughts on what he thought might help him remember. She listened as he talked and made notes. She knew it was crucial he finally had some answers, but it was also risky. Traumatic situations often led to memory loss and Joe was no exception. The counseling was helping, but doing what he was asking could potentially cause more harm than good.

"I can do it Joe, but you have to understand it is very risky. I think it should be used as a last resort, and please let your family know about it first."

Julie was genuinely concerned: she had seen so much progress and now that Sam was back in his life he was much happier. Dredging up

13

the past could send him back to square one, and that was something she didn't want to happen.

CHAPTER THREE

The winter storm that had been forecast had shifted direction, and Jason and Emily arrived mid-afternoon as planned. Sam didn't know whether to laugh or cry when she met them at the door, but cry she did.

"It is so good to see you two." she said through tears. "Oh my god, you must think I'm a wreck. Please, come in!"

Jason hugged her tightly. He missed her; they hadn't seen each other since the funeral. She had always been a part of their family, and losing both his dad and Sam was hard. At least now he had one of them back in his life.

Emily had missed her too; Sam had spent so much time with them over the years and shutting her out had been difficult. Emily had known what Sally was up to, and decided it was time to let them all know. She had her reasons for letting Sally know about the inheritance, and it had nothing to do with the money. She decided later would be soon enough - she wanted to see Uncle Joe.

"Okay you two, I have the suite above the garage ready and the spare room. The choice is yours."

Her cousins looked at each other and Jason said, "we'd both like to stay in the house with you if that's alright? I'll take the sofa."

Sam was surprised, but agreed. "Sounds good to me. I'll show you where you can put your things and then we'll go for a walk. Dad's meeting us halfway."

As Sam showed them the guest room she said, "you can put your things in here. I'll give you the tour later."

They walked to the conservatory, and Emily was in awe as they stepped inside (much like Sam had been when she first saw it). Joe was already there and Emily squealed "Uncle Joe!"

Joe embraced them and he couldn't help but notice how much Emily looked like Lenore. He could see some of Chad in her too, but any fool could see who her mother was. Jason was more of a mix between the two in looks, but his demeanor was all Chad.

"Shall we?" asked Sam as she removed her boots and coat. Her sandals were waiting for her and she slipped them on. "This is what your dad helped build. What do you think?"

"It's absolutely amazing!" Emily's eyes were as big as saucers as she looked around. "I can't believe he never told us about this place."
"Emily," Jason said, "he did. He just made us think it was all make-believe. Don't you remember?"

She thought for a moment, then realized he was right. Why hadn't she put two and two together before? The stories he told seemed like it was a far-fetched dream. She was upset with him for not sharing this with them, then realized perhaps it wasn't his to share. She had heard bits and pieces of conversations between her grandparents, and realized this must have been theirs at one time.

"Emily? You okay?" Joe was concerned; it had been quite some time since he had seen her phase out like that.
"Sorry," she said feeling a little embarrassed, "I was just thinking back, that's all. Didn't mean to scare you."
"Well Missy, back to reality," laughed Joe. "There's something I know your dad didn't tell you about." With that he and Sam cleared the doorway to the bunker. All they could do was follow; the ability to speak had suddenly escaped them.

Kody drove into Sam's yard and saw the unfamiliar SUV. He felt a twinge of jealousy, then remembered the conversation they had two days earlier. The SUV must belong to her cousins. A closer look confirmed his thoughts, as there was a Jones Landscaping and Garden Decor decal across the rear window. He walked to the front door and knocked. After waiting a minute or so, he knocked again. All he heard from inside was Bear barking.

"Where are they Bear?" he asked as he slowly opened the door.
"Woof, woof!" was Bear's reply.

He took off his boots and wandered through the house. He had never been there before without Sam, and wanted to see it all. He expected to find loose papers and notes on her desk, but was disappointed. (She made sure nothing was left out for prying eyes, even though she was the only one who lived there Her clients were her livelihood, and jeopardizing their trust in her was not something she wanted to do.) He was looking for dirt, and was quite upset she hid everything away.

As disgruntled as he was, and as much as he wanted to open her cabinets and check her computer files, he decided it was best to leave as he didn't know where she was or how soon she'd be back. He decided to leave it for another day, and got back in his truck, put it in reverse and turned around. "They must be at Joe's." he thought, and made a left turn as he left the drive.

Jason and Emily were amazed at the size of the underground quarters, and at how bright it was. Never before had they seen anything like it. The conservatory was breathtaking in itself, and being in the landscaping business they had seen and helped build a few over the years. Even with their background, they had never seen one quite like this. And never had they seen one built to disguise an underground facility.

17

Jason finally regained his ability to speak, but all he could utter was "Holy shit!"

Joe and Sam both laughed. "I do believe my first reaction was right along those lines Jason," said Sam. "Pretty phenomenal isn't it?"

Joe started to explain why it was so bright, because he knew that was one of the things they were wondering. He also went on to explain his "mix" and how beneficial it was to the plants.

"This is something your dad wanted you two to be a part of," he said as he looked at Jason and Emily "but he wanted to make sure the business he built for you was going to continue to thrive after you took over. In no way did he ever doubt your ability, but we all know how customers can be when a business changes hands. Some people will decide it just isn't the same and find another. You two have done a remarkable job of maintaining your client base and bringing in new business. We are now at the stage where the mix is just right, and it can now be bottled for use."

"You mean we are going to sell this stuff?" asked Emily.

"Not yet Emily. The first step is to use it in your own homes for your plants. Chad wanted to be sure it was going to work for everything before he made it available to the general public. I'm happy to say, we haven't killed anything yet.

After you use it for a month or two, you should notice a difference. When your season is back in full swing, you can begin using it in the business. It is not to be sold yet; rather it will become a part of your "added value" service. I will bottle some for each of you, as well as for each member of your staff. It is important they become familiar with it as well. Oh, and I do suggest before and after pictures of everything you use it on."

Jason thought for a minute. "Will there be enough for our customers? Our list gets longer every year."

"Don't worry Jason. We have a continuous supply here on the estate. You'll see where it comes from soon enough. Now, do you want to see the rest of this place?"

Joe and Sam showed them the rest of the bunker. They were amazed at the ingenuity their grandparents had, considering it was built in a time before so many technological advances had been made.

"This was built as a fallout shelter?" asked Emily.
"Yes, but it was never used for that. It never came to that. Instead of abandoning it, they decided to utilize it. It made a good retreat when severe weather was on its way.

Something in Sam's head clicked, and a light bulb went on. She couldn't wait to lay out a plan and get Joe's input. She took out her phone, opened the memo app, and began to make notes.

"How big is it?" Jason asked. He could see more doors and was curious to see what was behind them.
"Have a look - the doors are all unlocked," said Joe, motioning them in the general direction of the hall.

They all walked from room to room, and Joe reminisced about the few times they had taken refuge there during severe storms. His parents had stocked it with food and water; enough to last a week or more. They had always made sure Joe and Chad had plenty of things to do. The puzzles and games were still on a shelf in one of the rooms, and Sam could see tears in Joe's eyes when he wiped the dust off of the Monopoly game.

The beds were still made and the kitchen area was still stocked with utensils, cookware and dishes. There were also some preserves and dry goods, which Sam realized had been purchased the last time her and Joe had gone to the grocery store. She hadn't paid attention to it before, but he was rotating the provisions to ensure there was no danger of food poisoning should they ever need to utilize the bunker.

Jason and Emily were both amazed and hurt: amazed at the mere concept of the conservatory and its contents, and hurt because they had never been told of its existence.

Joe looked at his watch then said, "Shall we? I have chores to do and you two haven't seen the rest."

With that he led the way back up the stairs and into the main part of the conservatory. The door was closed and they all put on their winter wear once again. "I hope you two have mitts." Joe said as they walked out into the cold.

CHAPTER FOUR

Kody's truck was parked by the barn when they got to the yard. Joe smiled, "Well Sam, it looks like our workload is going to be easy today."

Emily caught sight of the alpacas right away. "Oh my God! What are those? They are so CUTE!"

"Haven't you ever seen an alpaca before?" Joe tried hard to suppress his laughter, but was failing miserably. Sam was stifling her own laughter and was glad Joe gave her an escape when he said "Go get Kody. Tell him not to be so stuck up."

Sam walked through the barn and found him with the yearlings. "Hey handsome! Did you miss me?"

He turned at the sound of her voice and she saw his face brighten. "Hi Babe! Of course I missed you! I stopped at your house first, but all I found was Bear. I thought you were here but came up empty handed, so decided to make myself useful."

"We appreciate that," she replied with a smile. "Now come on, Dad wants you to meet them."

Kody and Sam walked back through the barn hand in hand. Joe was telling the others about the alpacas, but stopped when he heard them. "Jason. Emily. I'd like you to meet Kody, my partner in crime and Sam's knight in shining Wranglers."

There were handshakes and "Nice to meet you's" all around, and

Emily felt her face flush when she realized she had looked at Kody a little longer than she should have. Joe was the only one who noticed, and he shook his head slightly when she looked at him. She knew no words were necessary; it was the same look her dad had given her when she ogled a couple of college students he had hired a few years earlier.

"Sam, do you want to take them upstairs and I'll help Kody with the rest of the chores." It was more of a suggestion than a question, and she knew saying anything but "Will do" was pointless. Even at her age she didn't argue with Joe; just as she had never refused Uncle Chad's requests.

"Okay guys, follow me," and she ran up the stairs.

Jason hit the top step first, and stopped so suddenly that Emily almost ran into him. Had it not been for the railing she would have surely fallen down several steps.

"Dammit Jason! What are you trying to do?" She was pissed at him for almost making her fall, but when she looked past him it was all but forgotten.

The loft looked like something right out of a textbook in Junior High. The Industrial Revolution came to mind when she saw the equipment lined up on the benches. Most of it was foreign to her, but she did recognize a weaving loom. It was very much like the one that had been set up in her fifth grade classroom.

Downstairs Kody and Joe finished the chores. "Watch her Kody. She has a tendency to try and unwrap what should only be eye candy for her."
"What are you talking about Joe?"
"Emily. Watch her. I saw the way she looked at you. If you want to have any further relationship with Sam, stay away from Emily. She has been warned, but that doesn't mean much."
"Oh, okay. She's one of those is she? Wants what she can't have, but then doesn't want it once she has it?"

"You got it!" Joe knew all about Emily's tendencies. Chad had spoken of some trouble she had caused between friends on more than one occasion. Joe knew (as Chad did) that she came by it honestly. He only hoped it was something she would tire of as she got older. Lenore had been a bit on the promiscuous side in her early twenties, but Chad had given her an ultimatum and she chose him.

Joe had a flashback of one night shortly after he met Sally. If he had known then what he knew now, he may have given in to Lenore's advances and innuendos. He was however, smart enough to know if he let anything happen between them, that Chad would take him out behind the barn. Chad was not one to be messed with when it came to his wife, and Joe wanted no part of his wrath.

Joe was back to reality when he heard them on the stairs. Kody had given him an "Are you okay?" look, but already knew the answer. He had known Joe long enough to know he was okay; but that didn't stop him from fearing one day he wouldn't be.

"Let's all go back to my house," said Sam. "I have supper in the oven."
"Now that sounds like a plan. I'm starving!"
Joe laughed. "Kody, you're always starving. If I didn't know better I'd swear you couldn't cook."

Sam hopped into Kody's truck with him and Jason and Emily rode with Joe. If it had been warmer he would have walked back, but it would be dark by the time he was ready to go home and the path wasn't lit.

As they all walked into Sam's house, Bear began to bark. Jason and Emily were surprised to hear a dog, because they had not seen any sign of one earlier. Sam opened Bear's kennel and he ran to meet their guests. Emily gasped when she saw him and grabbed onto Jason's arm. He laughed at his sister and knelt down to meet Bear at eye level. As ready as he thought he was, Bear still managed to

23

knock him over when he sniffed him. Jason lay on the floor laughing as Bear licked his face. Sam had never seen Bear do that before, and called him to the back door.

"Sorry Jason; I had no idea he was going to do that. He didn't hurt you did he?"
Jason laughed, "No, I'm fine. That'll teach me to take on a dog almost as heavy as I am. He must've figured I was an easy target since I was as low to the ground as he is. Mind you, he won't be that low to the ground for long."

After a supper of roast beef, scalloped potatoes, mixed vegetables and rhubarb crisp for dessert, Sam put water on for tea. Emily helped her clean up the kitchen while they chatted about work, old boyfriends and the upcoming hearing.

With the dishes put away and tea on a tray, Sam asked everyone to find a spot in the solarium. She handed each of them a cup of tea then got to the point. She had prepared a bit of a speech and wanted to get to the task at hand.

"First of all, I'm so glad you two are on board with us," she said as she looked at her cousins. "Without Uncle Chad here it just means we're going to have to work a little harder. You all know what my mother is claiming, and while I think it's a load of BS we still have to be prepared. Our futures depend on what happens in court. You two have your business and thankfully she can't touch that. This property staying in our family is my priority right now; we have a lot to lose if she gets her way. I am not giving up my dream without a fight."

Sam could feel tears welling up, but pressed on. "As you know, I wasn't told about Dad's accident; I just remember not seeing him anymore. I have an empty notebook for each of you to write down as much as you can remember, from as far back as you can remember. Kody, that means you too. You have known this family longer than I have, in a sense. I hate to be so bossy guys, but we really need to stop this in its tracks."

They each took their notebooks, and Sam gave them some key points to consider. These memories had to be documented, and the photos and newspaper clippings from the trunk were a good starting point.

"We have a few days to make some sense out of all of this. Keith will be coming over in the morning with a list of what he wants to know as well. Remember, he is a friend, but a lawyer first. Let him work his magic and we should have it in the bag. Everything we come up with can also be used in the divorce hearing, if it comes to that."

Sam suddenly felt very tired; the day had been busy. "Let's sleep on it and talk more over breakfast. Kody, will you be joining us or do you have to work?"

"I have to work, but I'll be out by five. I'll see what I can come up with. Oh, Heidi said she'd help in any way she could, and I think Julie is on board as well."

As he stood up to leave, he caught Emily looking at him. He pretended not to notice and said his goodnights. Sam walked him to the door and he kissed her, then whispered "there's more where that came from."

She had wanted him to stay, but knew it was best if he didn't. That kiss hadn't helped matters, and she had to settle down a bit before she went back to the others.

Sam awoke at seven the next morning and put on a pot of coffee. She hadn't slept very well even though she had felt very tired when she went to bed. She decided she'd start breakfast before she woke up her cousins. It had been almost midnight when they had said goodnight, and she wasn't sure how much later they had stayed up. They had learned a lot the previous day, so she didn't think sleep would have come easy to them either.

She was halfway through mixing the pancake batter when Jason walked into the kitchen, looking like he hadn't combed his hair or shaved in a week.

"Coffee?"

"Please! I'm going to need it today."

"You slept that well, eh?"

"I stayed up til almost three; I was making some notes. Once I started, more came to me. I tried to keep it in order, but you know how hard that can be. I hope it helps Sam."

"Thanks! Me too." Sam was worried. She wasn't sure what Sally had in her arsenal, but she hoped they had more. It basically was Sam's word against Sally's, but she hoped she remembered enough to make a difference. She knew they had one of the best lawyers in the province, but what if she had someone better?

"Anyone awake yet?" asked Joe as he opened the door.

"In here Dad! We saved you some coffee."

"Thanks! Hope you made it stronger than you usually do."

"An extra scoop just for you," Sam said with a smile as he walked into the kitchen. "Breakfast is almost ready."

"Did I hear someone say coffee?" asked Emily sleepily as she walked into the kitchen, still wearing her pajamas.

"Give me a minute and I'll make another pot. Dad just drained the last of it. Jason, could you get some plates out of the cupboard for me please?"

They chatted over a breakfast of pancakes, bacon, sausages and eggs. The upcoming court cases, the estate and the town itself were all topics of discussion. The townspeople would be able to fill in some of the blanks, and Sam suspected that many were anxiously waiting for the opportunity to talk about the estate they had kept hidden for so long. They decided that after their meeting with Keith, they would go into town and see Heidi and Julie. They had another list of people as well, but that would come in time.

Sam left the others after breakfast and went upstairs to shower. Bear followed her and wasted no time hopping (more like stepping) up on her unmade bed. He wasn't allowed on it often, but when he was he sprawled out and took up a good portion of it. Sam couldn't help but laugh when he opened one eye and looked at her as if to say "What?"

Keith arrived around 10 that morning, with briefcase and laptop in hand. He was going to do all he could to help them in court, but he had to go about it the right way; the formal way. He knew a lot about the family history, but he didn't know it all. He also didn't know all of the information he needed in terms of Sally's background and family history. That too was information they needed before they could proceed.

As they gathered in the solarium with coffee and notebooks in hand, Keith opened his briefcase and took out some files. He laid them on the coffee table and turned on his laptop.

"I'd like to get started, but first I want to say thank you for pulling together. Jason and Emily, I am happy you two are on board. I'm glad we could clear up the misconceptions you had about all of this. I didn't think you were being fair to Sam during the Reading of the Will."

Jason and Emily both felt the colour rise in their cheeks. "Yeah, we're really sorry about that," said Jason. "It was a shock to find out about it when we were still in shock over losing Dad. We didn't mean to sound so heartless and greedy."

"Either way, I'm glad to see you two here. I was hoping it was the grief talking and not greed. Your parents had differences of opinion when it came to raising you two, but it's good to know your dad instilled some solid values." With that, Keith smiled and everyone relaxed. "Now, lets get to work."

Keith went over the subpoena and quietly chuckled to himself. He was in disbelief that Sally would even attempt such a thing, but he knew they had to be prepared. He had seen people sue others for many different reasons, but this was one of the strangest and most selfish he had seen in a very long time.

He was also wise enough to know that occasionally cases that looked like a shoe-in went awry. He was not going to let some greedy bitch

27

take everything one of his best friends had worked so hard to build. Yes, Chad had parents that got him started, but it was he and Joe who spent the time and money to get it where it was at that point. It was, in a sense, a family heirloom that he was not going to give up without a fight; and it wasn't even his family.

"Okay everyone: I have looked it over, and although I don't see any problems with winning this case I also don't want to be unprepared. I think the more prepared we are the better the odds. I'm not too familiar with her lawyer's work, but I do know she tends to take on cases no one else will touch. And, she has, from my understanding, kicked ass on more than one occasion. I have never been against her in the courtroom, but a colleague has said she is ruthless."

Keith saw worry in the faces of his friends. He felt bad for causing more stress and worry, but if they were going to keep the estate and all of its assets, then they had to be ready for a fight.

"Now, what I need all of you to do is go through albums, scrapbooks, trunks, etc to see what part she played in all of this. If the judge thinks there is any of her time put in here she has a chance of getting something. She's claiming hardship and in my opinion is looking for a free ride. Joe, I'm presuming you have records of every penny you sent her?"

"I do," said Joe. "The last 10 years or so it has gone directly from my bank to hers. After the accident Chad helped me set it up that way. He said it would be best if I didn't have any face-to-face contact with her for awhile. Plus, he told me I had best cover my ass."

Sam giggled, "Yup, that sounds like Uncle Chad." Jason and Emily couldn't argue the point; they knew their father well. He was very much on the ball when it came to financial matters. He never did agree with Joe's choice for a wife and made sure he steered him in the right direction as far as record keeping was concerned. Chad knew it would come to this as soon as she found out Sam had inherited the estate, and he voiced his concerns to Keith. Keith was not at all surprised when he got the call for representation; it had only been a matter of time.

The next couple of weeks were spent going through the contents of the trunk, albums and old newspapers at the local library. Sam's researching skills proved very valuable and with the help of her cousins, Kody and several members of the community they felt they were as prepared as they were ever going to be. The night before Sam's court date was a sleepless one for her; more due to the fact that she had to face her mother than anything else. Sam was ready for her though, as there were things she learned about Sally and her side of the family she would have rather not known.

She also discovered she had relatives who had been trying to contact her for years; but all efforts were thwarted by Sally. Sam had cousins she had never met, and grandparents whom she had presumed were dead. It was only after Keith's suggestion to find out what she could that Sam even considered delving into the family history on her mother's side.

CHAPTER FIVE

Sam was ready to go much earlier than she needed to be, but she had spent the previous night worrying and going through all of what she had learned in her head. It was going to be a long day; she could feel it. She decided to opt for stronger coffee and a cinnamon raisin bagel for breakfast. The courthouse opened at 8 a.m. and she would have been there by 7 if it would have made a difference.

Joe arrived at 7:30 to pick her up, and she met him at the door. "Do you have everything?" he asked.
"Yes, do you?"
"I do." he said and they walked to his truck in silence, each lost in their own thoughts.

Jason, Emily, Kody, Heidi, Julie and several others met them at the courthouse. Keith was nowhere to be seen, but Sam had seen his vehicle in the parking lot. She presumed he was meeting with the judge prior to the start of the day. She knew there were other cases before hers, and he was there representing other clients as well. As she walked into the courtroom she saw the nameplate on the bench. It read "Judge Walker".

The court cases up to hers varied in nature. Some were for DUI, some for traffic violations and a vandalism charge. When her case was called, she was asked to proceed to the front of the courtroom. She had not seen Sally up to that point, but caught a glimpse of her out of the corner of her eye as she walked toward the judge. Keith had taken his place at a table to Sam's right as she faced the judge.

"State your name please," said the judge sternly.
"Samantha Jones."
"Do you have representation Ms. Jones?"
"I do Your Honour. Keith Macdonald is my representation."
"Mr. Macdonald, would you please step forward."

Keith left his spot at the table and joined Sam in front of the judge. "Ms. Jones, am I to understand you are here based on the claim of hardship by Sally Jones?"
"Yes Your Honour."

The judge looked over the documents he had in front of him, then said, "Mr. Macdonald; Ms. Jones, please have a seat at the table. Mrs. Jones, would you and your representation please step forward."

Sam watched Sally and her lawyer walk toward the judge, and saw Sally glare at her as she walked by. It was a look of pure hatred; as if Sam had been the one to initiate the situation.

"Mrs. Jones, let me get this straight. You are claiming hardship against your daughter; the daughter who has not lived under your roof for several years now, is that correct?"
"Yeah, that's right. She owes me!"

Judge Walker took a moment to collect himself; all he wanted to do at that point was to tell Sally to get the hell out of his courtroom and stop wasting everyone's time. This was one of the dumbest claims he had seen in his nearly 30 years of being a judge.

"Mrs. Jones, I would like to take a moment to inform you there is no valid reasoning for your claim. Your daughter inheriting an estate from her paternal grandparents does not give you just cause to lay claim to any part of it. It is my understanding that you receive a monthly income from your husband, which is more than enough to meet your basic needs. It is also my understanding that particular amount did not decrease when your daughter moved out on her own."

Sam and the others couldn't believe what they were hearing. Was it really going to end that quickly? Were they not even going to get the opportunity to present their defense? What had Keith said to the judge prior to the case being read?

"She owes me! I took care of her for over 18 years!" Sally's voice was raised; much like it had been when she called Sam shortly after she moved to the estate.

"Ms. Samson, please may I have a word with you? Mrs. Jones, you may be seated." Sally refused to move, and was once again told to take her seat. After a nod from her lawyer, she reluctantly stepped away from the bench and walked back to her chair.

Judge Walker turned to Sally's lawyer, "Ms. Samson, I am very disappointed to see you have even allowed this case to reach my bench. I do not know what you told your client she would gain, but you know as well as I do this is a wrongful lawsuit. Case dismissed!"

"What?! She owes me! I took care of her for most of her life. I gave her life! If it wasn't for me she wouldn't even be here!"
"Mrs. Jones, your time here is over. Please stop disrupting my courtroom or I will have you removed. I usually don't get involved in anything beyond my verdict, but I must say in my almost 30 years of being a judge, you have attempted one of the lowest, most ridiculous lawsuits in legal history. Now leave my courtroom before I charge you with contempt."

Sally was livid; her face reddened and she shouted, "They will pay! They owe me for all I've done for them! How dare they think they can live out there and not give me any of it. He owes me half of it!" She looked at Joe and screamed, "Just you wait - the divorce will leave you with nothing! Do you hear me? NOTHING!"

"Bailiff, please remove this woman from my courtroom and escort her to a holding cell."

Judge Walker had had enough. He had seen a lot in his years as a judge, but this woman took the cake. He was not going to be responsible for any damage she might do to others in her present state, so he had two female bailiffs escort her down the hall.

"Ms. Jones and Mr. Macdonald, you are free to go. There will be no further action concerning this case. As for the divorce mentioned, I will review the paperwork when it comes across my desk. You will be contacted by my office at that time. Good luck."

Sam and the others were in shock; both because of the fact that the case was dismissed and the outburst from Sally. Joe hadn't realized up until that point that she no longer cared about him or Sam. He suspected she only considered him a cheque with a heartbeat, but to say what she did about Sam was completely uncalled for. As they walked out into the cold February air, they could still hear Sally screaming obscenities at them and the bailiffs. A few moments later, there was the sound of a siren and the ambulance came to a screeching halt outside the courthouse. It was a day they would not soon forget.

It had been decided the day before that no matter what happened in court, everyone was to meet back at the estate. The events of the day had been both trying and disturbing, and that had left Sam with more questions than answers. She still couldn't believe her mother had freaked out the way she did, especially in the courtroom. Did she think she was going to gain sympathy from the judge, or was she acting up just to get her way? Either way, Sam didn't think Sally was prepared to be taken away to the mental health ward of the hospital, where she would be held for observation for at least 48 hours.

Keith joined them and stated Sally's lawyer's credentials were going to be put up for review. Judge Walker was not putting up with any more bullshit cases, and had given her an ultimatum. It wasn't often that the judge meddled in the lives of lawyers, but this particular case had him frazzled. She had to either agree to a full review of her caseload since she passed the Barr Exam, or be disbarred. She liked the perks of being a lawyer, and for the most part she was on the up and up. She took on cases such as this one when she felt she needed more than what her usual clientele provided. Her risk taking put her career on the line this time; and she was not happy.

Sally's outburst was the main focus of the conversation for a little while. None of them had ever thought the case would take the turn it did. They had anticipated a longer time in front of the judge or at the very least a chance to say their piece. Greed had most definitely taken over, as had the possibility of serious mental health issues. Sally had been depressed and on medication for many years; perhaps there were some serious side effects after taking them for an extended period of time.

Emily was most troubled by the outburst, which had surprised Sam. "Okay Emily, spill it!"

Everyone looked at Sam in both wonder and disbelief. What in the world was she getting at?

"Are you sure you want to hear this Sam? Do you really think now is a good time?"
"Now is the perfect time Emily. Tell everyone what you know about Mom and why you were the one filling her in on all of the little tidbits of information."

The others were surprised. What had Sam found out in the last couple of weeks that she wasn't letting anyone know about?

"If you say so Sam." She turned toward the others and started to explain. "Dad asked me to make Sally think I was on her side. It was the only way he could really see what was going on with her. Uncle Joe, I feel terrible for not filling you in on it, but Dad said to just play it by ear. He was worried about you and was afraid you'd do something harsh.
He knew you weren't in the best health or state of mind after the accident, so he told me to keep things the same between her and I. We always got along, and that was why he picked me to dig up some dirt. I know that doesn't sound like Dad, but he had the best of intentions."

She looked at the others and continued, "He knew Sally was a nutcase, and knew she was waiting for Uncle Joe to die so she could have the life insurance which was a hefty two million dollars. When he pulled through, she was very upset. She had tried to mess with meds at the hospital a couple times, so she was no longer allowed to go see him. Sam, the only bad part about that was you weren't allowed to go see him either. Dad wanted to take you, but she wouldn't allow it."

Joe was in disbelief. His wife had tried to kill him? Why had Chad never said anything to him about it? Was he afraid he'd take matters into his own hands?

"The money for Sam was set up to be put into two accounts; one for day to day expenses, the other for college. Sally managed to drain the college fund by pleading a hard luck story to the bank, and Dad found out about it after the fact. She hadn't known he knew the bank manager; the bad part was they hadn't known each other well enough to catch the scam in action. After that happened, I became Dad's "little spy", which I was very good at. He had told me, that no matter what happened to him, I was to keep an eye on her. I took my job very seriously, and after he died I made sure to "leak" information every once in awhile just to keep her interested. He was afraid that she would hook up with some millionaire and never be seen again. I do have to say though, anyone with money didn't stick around long. She is not very good at playing it cool."

"Is that why she went out so much when I was little? Because she was 'looking' for a man that would give her everything she wanted?"

"Yes Sam, I do believe that is exactly the reason. Uncle Joe gave her what he could, but she was never satisfied. She always wanted more, but never wanted to do anything in return. It never took the men she went out with very long to figure her out. They would buy her dinner, take her shopping when she wanted to go or buy her jewelry, but when she refused to let them visit her at home or let them meet you they would carry on."

Joe's head was starting to throb. He had suspected she was going out with other men, but didn't expect the one-sided effort. As he thought back, he realized that was how she got him too. She was very pretty, but not once did she offer to buy a meal or tickets to a movie. It was a time when women insisted on paying for something at least once in awhile, but she had never offered. She seemed to adore him and was available for every date he asked her out on. He had fallen head over heels in love with her, and married her against his family's wishes. They had seen her for who she was, but he was oblivious to her faults and insisted on being with her.

"Dad? Dad!" Sam reached him just as he went over. Keith and Kody helped her lay him down on the floor, and she put a pillow under his head. "What's wrong with him?" There was fear in her eyes; she couldn't lose him now, not after she had just gotten to know him again.

"Easy Sam. He'll be okay. Just give him a few minutes. This is a lot for him to take in all at once; it has been a very stressful day for everyone." Kody reassured her again all would be fine. Tears were streaming down her face as she watched him lying on the floor. Keith called the ambulance, just to be sure there was nothing more serious going on and Kody kept checking his heart rate. He was afraid something like this might happen, but he didn't want to worry Sam by mentioning it before. Joe was a tough old bugger and had been through much worse; there was no way this was going to slow him down for long.

"Kody! What's wrong with him?" Sam was worried, scared and feeling guilty for getting Emily to tell them what she knew about Sally. Had she known something like this was going to happen she wouldn't have pushed the issue.

"It's okay Sam, he'll be fine. It has been a rough day; hearing all he has today has put him in shut-down mode. It hasn't happened since shortly after Chad died, but before that it was several times after the accident. Keith, is there an ETA on the ambulance?"

"They'll be here in a few minutes. Joe! Can you hear me? Joe!" Keith gently shook Joe's shoulder, but got no response. "Son of a bitch!"

Emily had left the room crying, and Jason had gone after her. She felt responsible for Joe blacking out, and was very afraid he might not come back. "Easy Sis. He'll be fine."

Back in the solarium Sam was sitting on the floor by her dad, watching him to make sure he was still breathing. He wasn't moving, nor was he responding to their voices. He looked very white, but she didn't know what had caused him to pass out.

A couple minutes later she heard the ambulance and could see the flashing lights. Keith met the two attendants at the door and they rushed in with bags and knelt down on the floor beside him. Kody had moved the coffee table and anything else that may be in their way so they had room to work.

"What happened?" asked one of them as he took Joe's vitals and called his name.

"We have had a very exhausting and stressful day. He just found out some "history" if you will, and passed out. No signs of anything awry, just over. Sam caught him as he went over and we eased him onto the floor." Kody had taken charge of answering questions; Sam was getting very emotional and was having a difficult time getting the words out.

One EMT continued with questions while the other went out to get the stretcher. They asked all the usual questions in terms of health, heart problems, allergies to medications and more. They took his blood pressure and hooked him up to a heart monitor. No matter what they did, he remained unresponsive. Sam was terrified; she had never seen anyone pass out like that and not regain at least some level of consciousness after a few minutes.

CHAPTER SIX

Sam rode in the ambulance with Joe and Kody, Jason and Emily followed in Kody's truck. Keith spent a few extra minutes putting Bear in his kennel and making sure all was secure before he left. Mittens had hid under the sofa in the living room when the EMTs arrived, so Keith tried to coax him out. After several failed attempts, he decided to leave the kitten be and made sure the door to the laundry room was open.

The ride to the hospital was fast, but not fast enough for Sam. She had no idea what was wrong, but had a nagging feeling there was something she hadn't been told. Joe had still not responded to her or the EMT, and that worried her to death. She was afraid for him, and very angry at her mother. She hoped Sally was in a straight-jacket in a room alone, because that was where she deserved to be. Sam wasn't a vindictive person, but after the outburst she had seen earlier she had lost all respect for her mother (not that there had been much in the past few years anyhow). She wanted Sally to suffer, and Joe to regain consciousness.

When they arrived at the hospital there was a bustle of activity and she tried to stay out of the way. The EMTs had taken Joe into the ER and she tried to stay close by, but not get in the way. The nurses that came in started asking her questions and she answered as best as she could. She really wished the others would get there soon; Kody seemed to know more about Joe's medical history than anyone else. She presumed it was because he helped Joe on the estate. The staff was baffled as to why he wasn't coming out of it; vital signs were almost normal considering the activity that had just gone on.

The doctor walked in as the EMTs were taking out their equipment. The room was big, but not big enough to have a gurney and so many extra people. The nurses had switched the leads from the ambulance monitor to the ER EKG machine, and had started an IV (standard procedure).

"I'm Dr. Green. What do we have here?" Once again the questions were asked about medical history, allergies to food or medication, etc. Sam answered the doctor to the best of her ability, and let him know about the accident that had left Joe in ICU several years earlier.

Dr. Green made notes on the chart and examined Joe from head to toe. He looked in his eyes, ears, tested reflexes and checked for any signs of recognition or alertness. He was seeing a body that was relatively healthy, but feared something terrible had happened inside Joe's brain.

"What's wrong with him? Is he having a heart attack?" Sam pleaded.
"I can tell you his heart is fine, but I don't like the fact he is completely unresponsive. Have you ever seen this happen before?"
"I have," Kody said as he walked into the room. "He came out of it within a few minutes last time with no ill effects. Has he responded at all this time?"
"Nothing. And you are?" asked Dr. Green.

"I'm Kody; I help Joe out on the farm with the animals. We spend a lot of time together, but I have never seen him out for this long. It has been several months since this happened, and last time he had just found out his brother died."
"I see. Has he had previous episodes when this has happened?" Dr. Green was trying to get as much information as possible, but had a bad feeling his suspicions were right.
"I already told you he had severe head injuries several years ago!" Sam was in tears and very upset.
"Easy Sam," said Kody. "Dr. Green is just trying to do his job. He's trying to help your dad, but if you freak out at him it makes it hard to do."

Sam was taken aback; Kody had never spoken to her like that before. The whole experience was overwhelming. She knew everyone was at wits end, but she couldn't help the feelings of despair and anxiety.

"Let me make a call to the University," said Dr. Green. "I'll be back as soon as I can."

"Kody, what's wrong with him? Why won't he wake up?"

"I don't know Sam. He has never been out this long before. I hope they can figure this out before there is any permanent damage."

Dr. Green walked back in the room. "I have the air ambulance on the way. The specialist I talked to will be waiting for him and they have a CT scan and MRI scheduled."

"MRI?" asked Kody. "He was shot several years ago and I'm pretty sure there is still shrapnel in him."

"Oh? Okay, I'll let them know. In the meantime I need to know what he is taking for medications and if he has consumed any alcohol with it."

"No medications aside from the occasional pain killers, and as for alcohol none that we know of. We spent the day in court then went back to my place, where he collapsed." Sam was trying hard to keep it together, but felt as if she was failing miserably.

"I'm afraid there is no room in the helicopter for anyone besides the patient and staff. They will take care of him and you can meet them there. Drive safe; I don't want to see either of you coming back in here in an ambulance." With that the doctor left the room and the nurses began getting Joe ready for transport.

Sam stood beside him for a few minutes crying silently. "I love you Dad. Stay with us."

Jason and Emily were just inside the door, and Jason said, "We'll meet you at the hospital there. You can stay with us as long as you need to. He'll be okay Sam."

She watched them walk away, and then turned back toward the bed. The nurses had just moved him onto the gurney and were waiting for the air ambulance attendants when the convulsions started.

"Oh my God! DAD!"

"Son of a bitch!" muttered Kody. "Come on Sam, let's give them some room." They stepped out of the room just as the air ambulance team arrived.

After what seemed like hours (but it had only been about 15 minutes) Dr. Green emerged from the room, with a solemn look on his face. "He's stable, for now. There is a neurology team waiting at the University for him. They will be able to help him and let you know what is going on. Best of luck to you."

Sam and Kody watched as the team wheeled Joe down the hallway toward the Heli-Pad, not knowing if they would see Joe alive again. Sam was scared, and riddled with guilt for bringing up so much of the past; a past Joe had only suspected. She felt solely responsible for his condition, and told Kody so.

"Sweetie, you can't blame yourself. We don't know what else has been going on with him; he is stubborn as a mule and I wouldn't doubt that he hasn't told us as much as he should have. Let's not jump to conclusions and just get going. He'll be there long before us, so hopefully they have some answers by the time we get there."

Sam called Keith to let him know what was happening, and asked if he could take care of things at least for the night. She then called Parker and the others, and asked if they could be on standby in case she needed some help. Being the good friends that they were, they agreed. Parker had been waiting for an opportunity to leave the city for a little while, but hadn't had a valid reason. He now had one, and decided whether or not Joe was okay he would still go out to help Sam. "Just say the word Sam. I'll be there."

CHAPTER SEVEN

The drive to the University seemed to take forever. They rode mostly in silence, each lost in their own thoughts. Sam felt guilty for not considering Joe's feelings when she had Emily fill everyone in on what she knew, and Kody was replaying the scenario over and over trying to figure out what they might have missed.

"Didn't Joe say he had a headache today? Was there something going on earlier that we missed?"
"I can't remember Kody. I was so caught up in my own thoughts this morning I may have missed him saying anything; that is, if he did say anything."
"I'll let the doctor know when we get there; maybe it will help them figure this out. Sam, I'm so sorry this happened. I don't know what to say or do right now."
"You and me both! Do you think this was just too much for him to cope with? Or is there more to it than we think? I'm going to call Julie; maybe she can let us in on some of his secrets."
"You know she won't do that; she takes patient confidentiality very seriously Sam. Mind you, if there is any indication it will make a difference she might go against her own rules."

Sam made the call to Julie, and was surprised to learn that Joe had complained of a headache the previous day. Julie didn't usually say much to family members in terms of her patients or "clients" as she like to call them, but this case was different. "I can't say much right now Sam, but let me know how he is. Please keep me updated, no matter what."

Kody found a parking spot and he and Sam rushed into the hospital emergency department looking for a familiar face, whether it was an air ambulance attendant or her cousins.

"Sam, over here!" Sam turned toward the voice and was relieved to see Jason.

"Where is he? Have they done anything yet?" Sam could feel herself reaching the point of hysteria again, and did all she could to suppress it. She didn't do well in intense situations like this, but she knew she had to keep it together. The last thing she wanted was to be hauled away like her mother had been earlier that day. The thought itself was sobering; had it only been earlier that day? It seemed like an eternity ago.

"He's in the CT now. They wouldn't tell me much, but did say he had a seizure on the way here."

"Oh my God Kody! Another one?" Sam was not liking how this was turning out. She had high hopes that all would be well by the time they arrived at the hospital, or that it was all a very bad dream.
"What do you mean 'another one'?", asked Jason. "What happened after we left the hospital?"

Kody relayed the events prior to Joe being airlifted. "Dammit! I thought those days were long gone!" Jason recalled the weeks after the accident, where the seizures were a regular occurrence. He had hoped, for Joe's sake, they wouldn't return. He recalled how frustrated Joe would get; perhaps there was a trigger of some sort that no one else picked up on. Oh, how he wished his dad was there; he would know all of the answers.

Jason cursed under his breath. He wanted to go to the prison where Joe's assailants were still serving time and beat the living shit out of every one of them. He was thankful for the one who had the balls to spill the beans about the attack, even though it cost him his life. He sincerely hoped the others would rot in jail; he felt no remorse at that moment for his thoughts. He was mad, and would do anything at that point to bring Uncle Joe back to the present.

A nurse from behind the desk walked over to Jason and the others. "The doctor will see you now; follow me." She led them into a room that was just down the hall from the CT Scanner. "The doctor will be in shortly," she said and left the room.

Sam looked around, and saw the room was close to the size of her living room, with probably just as much furniture. There was a sofa, an armchair and a loveseat, along with a table with several magazines. She took the opportunity to sit down, because she felt if she didn't she would be laid out on the floor. The others followed suit and waited for the doctor.

They didn't have to wait long for the neurologist and a nurse. "I prefer to meet new people under different circumstances, but it seems this is the only way I meet anyone new. I'm Dr. Henry Walsh and this is Debbie. I usually ask people to sit down at this point, but you seem to be one step ahead of me." Dr. Walsh was trying hard to lighten the mood just a little, but felt the others knew the news wasn't good. "I'm afraid the prognosis isn't good. There are some lesions in his brain, which most likely were caused by the head injuries sustained during the attack. We also found what appears to be a new lesion, which is possibly the cause of the latest episode. I went through his medical charts and there have definitely been some changes in his brain since his last scans. I would like your consent to operate to see exactly what is going on. The seizures are a major concern, especially since they came on so suddenly and with such severity after all this time."

Sam was in disbelief. How could someone who was doing so well go downhill so quickly? "Whatever it takes Dr. Walsh. We just want him back."

"I would like to tell you everything is going to be okay Ms Jones, but I can't do that. The damage may be too severe, especially with the latest head injury."

"What do you mean by "latest head injury"? Kody questioned. "His head injuries were sustained years ago."
"I'm afraid there is evidence of a more recent one. Has he mentioned

falling or hitting his head on anything in the past week?"

"No," they all answered at once.

"I have a sneaky suspicion he may have had a seizure recently and hit his head. Either that or he fell. I'm going to do an EEG before I do surgery, just to see what is going on inside his head. I want to avoid cutting into him if I can, but I'm afraid I may not have a choice."

"You can go see him if you wish."said Debbie. "It will help if he knows you are there. You can be there during the EEG; it will help with brain activity. He won't be able to answer questions, but if he hears familiar voices it should relay some regular brain function. We don't usually allow anyone else in the room while this is being done, but in this case we'll make an exception."

Sam and the others went into the room Joe was in. The EEG machine was nearby, and the technician was getting ready to hook it up. "I'm going to ask you some questions and I want you to answer to the best of your ability. The machine will pick up any brain activity as we go through the test. There will be times when I will need complete silence as well in order to monitor the activity at rest."

The test took about twenty minutes, and they took turns answering questions about Joe's past as best they could. As they talked about past events and the events of the day, the technician made notes. It was difficult for Sam to refrain from asking questions, but she knew the tech couldn't answer them anyway. They would just have to wait for the doctor to look at the results.

Sam and the others anxiously awaited the doctor's diagnosis. They knew it wasn't looking good, but still hoped Joe would be okay. Hope was all they had at this point, as he wasn't showing any signs of being with them or even knowing they were there.

They stayed with him, watching for signs of voluntary movement or attempts to speak. They watched to see if his eyes opened or if he moved his feet or hands. The night wore on, and there was still no sign that Joe was with them at all.

At 2 AM the doctor came into the room, and he could see the worry and concern in their eyes and faces. He knew he would soon be bombarded with questions, so he started to tell them what he learned from the tests.

"I'm afraid the tests didn't give me the results I had hoped for. I'm not seeing regular brain activity, but there are signs he still has a fighting chance. I am going to go ahead with the surgery, if that's okay with you?"

"Of course it's okay with us," said Sam. "We don't want to lose him and will do whatever it takes to help him." Tears were streaming down her face, and she thought about how close they were to losing him forever. She was not a religious person by any means, but she prayed they could have more time with him. She was not ready to say goodbye; not after it taking so many years for her to finally get to know him. She cursed her mother for driving him away, and for causing the stress and anxiety they had all suffered in recent weeks.

"I'm going to need some forms signed before I can proceed with the surgery. I'll do my best to help him folks."

Sam read over the forms and signed them. It was heartbreaking to face the reality she may no longer have the father she had been kept away from for so many years. She knew there was nothing she could do but wait.

The nurses prepped Joe for surgery, and Sam spent a few moments alone with him.

"Dad, I hope you can hear me," she said in a cracked voice. "I was so happy to find you again; to know you were okay. Please be okay after this; we have so much to catch up on and there is so much I have to learn about the alpacas. I love you!"

As they wheeled him off to surgery, Sam cried into Kody's shirt. No one knew the outcome and what the surgery would bring. She silently prayed that he would be alright, and that there would be no long term effects. She also thought the unthinkable: if he was going to remain in a vegetative state with no glimmer of improvement, she prayed he would pass away. She couldn't see him suffering and laying in a hospital bed for the next 20 or 30 years.

CHAPTER EIGHT

The clock in the family waiting room ticked loudly, and that was often the only sound there was. Each was lost in their own thoughts and worries; each hoping the surgery would shed some light on the prognosis, if nothing else.

Sam was afraid of losing her father, but did not want to see him suffer either. She recalled a conversation they had recently had, and she wondered if he had perhaps known something was awry. They had been out in the barn and somehow the conversation had turned toward illness and death. She hadn't thought much about it then, but now looking back she realized he was perhaps trying to tell her something.

He had talked about not wanting her to sign any resuscitation forms should he be involved in an accident or suffer a severe stroke; he didn't want to be a burden to her or anyone else. He had been in that position before, but managed to survive and go on to live a relatively normal life. He feared the next time he wouldn't be so lucky.

As she replayed the conversation in her head, she realized it was entirely up to her to decide his fate. She wasn't sure if she wanted that responsibility; it was a huge load to carry and she would have to live with the results for the rest of her life. Depending on the outcome of the surgery, she would talk to Keith to see who Joe had named as his Power of Attorney. She feared it was her.

Kody had gone to a nearby coffee shop and brought back coffee, sandwiches and some doughnuts. "If we're going to be any help to Joe, we have to eat something."

Sam then realized none of them had eaten much since breakfast. The day seemed almost surreal to her, as the events that had unfolded were as whacky as a scripted television show. Who needed reality TV when there were days like that one had been. A court appearance, her mother being escorted from the courtroom and a trip to the emergency room which ended in an air ambulance trip and brain surgery. She felt overwhelmed and tried hard to put it all into perspective. She was glad her mother was in a secured facility; if not she truly felt she would think nothing of going to her house and letting her have it.

As the clock ticked on, they sat mostly in silence. The food had helped a little, as they weren't feeling quite so ill any more. Sam's headache was slowly dissipating to a dull ache, and she knew it was lack of food and proper hydration that had caused it.

Five hours after Joe was wheeled into the operating room, the doctor came into the waiting room. They all stood as he walked in the door, but he motioned for them to sit down again. Kody felt a sense of dread; he was not looking forward to what he thought the doctor had to say.

"I have done a thorough exam and found more than I thought I would. It appears the CT didn't pick up some of the damage to his brain, which was caused by bleeding from a recent head injury. What I don't understand is why it wasn't clear during the scans, unless it started to bleed after the scans were finished. If that's the case, I am completely baffled as to why that would happen. It may remain a medical mystery, but I prefer a logical explanation for every problem that comes through my doors. The brain is very complex and over-analysing will surely drive anyone nuts."

"Is he going to be okay? What does his future hold?" Sam wasn't sure if she should have asked the latter question, but it was too late now.

"He is still critical, but stable. The bleeding has been stopped and the pressure has been relieved from his brain, at least for now. I have him in a medically induced coma for now, even though he was in that state before surgery. Now that the pressure is relieved, I don't want him waking up and not knowing what is going on. His breathing is being assisted for the time being as well, since the bleeding did affect his respiratory function.

I don't want to give you folks false hope, but I also don't want you to think you've lost him either. Recovery from something like this can take months; time will tell all. We're going to let him sleep for a few more hours so we can get a baseline for his vitals, then we'll see if we can take him off the respirator. It looks like you all could use some sleep too."

"Can we see him?" asked Sam. "Even for just a few minutes?"

"Yes, but only one at a time for now. I must warn you, he doesn't look like the man who went into surgery. We had to shave his head and he's bandaged. There's also a tube draining fluid from his brain."

Sam was the first to walk into the ICU. She was met by the nurse who was assigned to him, and she explained she would be his nurse for the next 8 hours. Sam was glad she wasn't completely alone in the room with her dad; at least with the nurse there she could shake the eerie feeling she had. She had been warned about his appearance, but she was still not prepared to see him lying in bed. His head was wrapped in gauze, there was a tube coming out and fluid was draining into a small bag. His face looked ashen and the fluid they had been giving him through IV had puffed up his face; or perhaps it was swelling caused by the surgery itself. Not in a million years did she expect to see him in this condition. She had seen pictures of him after his accident but this was different; this was real.

The respirator was keeping his breathing regular, and there were wires connected to both him and the monitors. He had an oxygen saturation monitor taped to his finger, and a blood pressure cuff on his arm. The monitor showed heart rate, oxygen levels and blood pressure (which was being monitored every 15 minutes). It was all Sam could do to keep from running out of the room crying; she knew her place was in that room even though every fiber of her being was telling her to leave. As she reached out to take his hand, she saw the bag hanging from the bed, which meant a catheter as well. He was not going to be a happy camper when he woke up (if he woke up).

"Dad, can you hear me? I'm here now. Jason, Emily and Kody are all outside waiting to see you too. What happened to you? Why didn't you tell us anything was wrong?"

Sam's eyes filled with tears once again; tears she didn't think she had left. There was no response from Joe, but she didn't expect there to be. He was, after all, in a coma. She watched the monitors as she talked to him, looking for any signs of irregularities that may be a signal of him knowing she was there. She saw none. She couldn't stand it any longer; she had to leave the room before she passed out. She leaned over and kissed him on the cheek. "I love you Dad."

The others each took a turn to go in and see Joe, but they didn't spend more than a couple minutes each with him. Emily was once again in tears when she came out; she just couldn't shake the feeling that she was responsible for the position he was in. She knew what she had revealed had to be done, but if she had known his condition she would have left well enough alone.

Dr. Walsh returned and asked them to follow him back to the waiting room. "I will keep him asleep for a few more hours if you want to go get some rest. I know you have all had a tough day. Do you have somewhere to stay, or should we see if there's an available suite in the hostel?"

"My sister and I live here," replied Jason. "We'll be fine, but thank you for the offer."

"Okay. We know how difficult it is for some when family members are flown in. I'll call the contact number when I am ready to wake him up. Right now, letting him rest is the best thing to do. He has his very own nurse and she will keep a good eye on him so you guys can get some rest. I'll see you in a few hours."

The four of them left the hospital, and Kody and Sam followed Jason and Emily to Jason's house. Sam knew where it was, but decided it was probably easier for them to follow instead. She feared she would get them lost in her state of mind, and she didn't want to do that.

Kody called Keith when they got to Jason's and gave him an update on what was happening.

"Shit!" said Keith when Kody told him about Joe needing surgery and being in ICU. "What the hell happened when we weren't looking? Just like him to not say anything to anyone."

"Could you also call Julie; I think she needs to know. Maybe he has told her more than he has told us. Sam's friends will go look after things out there if you and Julie want to come to the hospital. I really hope she agrees to breaking some doctor/patient confidentiality. If he has said anything to her about this, we need to know. Could you call her and get back to me as soon as you talk to her?"
"You betcha! I'll call her right away; she usually doesn't have clients until 10, so I should be able to catch her." With that, Keith hung up the phone. Julie's number wasn't one he had in his speed dial, so he had to look it up.

"Hello?" said Julie on the second ring.

"Julie, it's Keith. I'm sorry to bother you at home, but it is very important.

"What's wrong Keith? Anything I can do to help?"

"I'm so glad to hear those words. Yes, as a matter of fact there is. Are you sitting down?, because what I have to say isn't pleasant at all."

"I am now. Spill it Keith." Julie had a bad feeling, but she would never have expected to hear what she did.

"There is no easy way to say this, so I'm just going to get it over with. Joe is in the University in a coma. I must add it is a medically induced coma, and we were hoping you could shed some light on the subject."

"Oh my God! What happened?!"

Keith explained the events of the previous afternoon and evening to her. She had known about the courthouse commotion, because she had been there but aside from that all she knew was what Sam had told her the day before. She hadn't realized he hadn't regained consciousness yet..

"Is he going to be okay? I just can't believe that happened!"
"We honestly don't know Julie," said Keith sadly. "We were hoping you could help us out. Has Joe said anything to you about falling or hitting his head lately? Or having a seizure?"

There was silence on Julie's end, and she was trying to find the words that she knew she must say. "You know that what Joe tells me in my office stays in my office. I can't reveal anything."

Keith suddenly found himself getting angry, but tried hard to hide it. "Julie, he is in very bad shape. The doctors can't figure it out, so please, if he has said anything to you, tell us or tell the doctor. You can ride with me if you like; I'll be going up as soon as my replacements arrive."
"Replacements? Where are you?"
"I stayed at the estate to keep an eye on Bear and Mittens. No one had any idea how long they'd be when the ambulance left. It was a good thing I did stay, since they all ended up going to the University. Sam's friends will come and look after things here if you want to go up."
"Okay, let me make some calls. I have a few clients today that I'll have to reschedule."
"Thanks Julie. Let me know as soon as you can. I think I'll go up either way, so I'll give Kody a call."

Keith called Kody back and told him that he hadn't learned much, but that she was most likely going to go with him.

"Okay. I'll let Sam know and she can call her friends. They'll look after the place for her. Maybe you can make them a chore list while you're waiting, if you could please. Send me a copy of it and I'll double-check to make sure nothing has been forgotten.

Keith hung up the phone and wondered what he would ever do without his smartphone. His life was in that phone, and emailing a list to Kody from it was just one of the things he could do with it. How had he ever gotten along without one? he wondered.

CHAPTER NINE

With Parker and Simon settled in at Sam's, Keith headed home to shower, change and pack for at least a couple of days. Julie had agreed to go with him, but she still wasn't revealing much in the line of what he wanted to know. He hoped the two hour drive would make her talk. He understood the circumstances of doctor/patient confidentiality, but this was a life or death situation. The doctors (at least) had to know what was going on with Joe.

Keith parked in front of Julie's home/office and waited. She told him she would watch for him, and that there was no need for him to go to the door. He saw her emerge from the house in less than a minute, with a carry-on bag over her shoulder and her purse in hand.

"You can put that in the back seat. It will keep your toothpaste from freezing." Keith said. "Hop in!"

Julie got in the front seat and said, "thanks for calling me. Joe was supposed to come and see me today, so my client list wasn't as full as I thought. The others were okay with me cancelling for a few days. I hope I can be of some help. I didn't mean to sound so insensitive earlier today, but it was quite a shock. I also don't expect someone of your education to be asking me for confidential information."

"I don't make a habit of it Julie, but it may be all we've got to work with. The rest know nothing about any falls, seizures or anything of the sort. We were really hoping you could shed some light on the subject. We know he sees you regularly, and appreciate all you have done for him. I don't think he'll hate you for telling on him." Keith managed to smile slightly, and Julie felt more at ease.

She had met Keith several years ago, and saw him occasionally in town. She wasn't in his social circle, so really didn't know what to expect. She had considered passing on the invitation to ride with him to the city, but decided Joe needed her more. She put her insecurities aside and told herself to suck it up and put her big girl panties on. As educated as she was, she still had some of the same old personal issues that she had in school so many years before.

Julie and Joe had more than a therapist/client relationship; a relationship no one else knew about. It had begun on a strictly professional level, but as the years went on they found they had some common ground. Joe had been taking his wedding vows seriously, even though he hadn't spent any time with Sally for several years. He was determined to stay faithful to her, but Julie changed all that.

She had a way of getting people to talk - it was, after all, her specialty. As their sessions went on and Joe remembered bits and pieces of his past, he started to think more about his future. Did he really want a wife who didn't care about him? He had suspicions about her infidelity, but never called her on it. It was just easier to give her the $2500 each month (pretty decent for someone who did nothing in return) than to start divorce proceedings. He had his disability pension after the accident to live on, plus he had collected a sizeable sum of money from insurance. It was the insurance money which had been paying Sally's bills all these years, as well as for Sam's care. Sally had not known about the insurance money, which was just as well. He had feared if she did, she would have demanded half of it. He had to live too, so it was not something he was going to tell her about until he had to.

Julie was not interested in Joe for his insurance windfall (if you could call it that, considering the hell he had gone through to get it); she had grown to love him for who he was. His biggest worry was Sam's well-being, but at least he had Chad to keep him updated on her. He was proud of her accomplishments in school, and who she had become. He knew he had been wrong in not contacting her as soon as he was able, but he wanted to protect her from seeing him in his wounded state. As the years went on his physical wounds healed, but the psychological and mental damage could not be undone. It was something he was going to have to live with for the rest of his life, and many times he hadn't been sure he could do that.

Julie didn't usually let clients call her after hours, but as time went on she let Joe call her when he needed someone to talk to. She knew he had Chad, but sometimes there were topics of interest he couldn't discuss with Chad, especially where Emily was concerned. Joe worried about his niece; but worried more about what she may say to Sally since they seemed to have a special friendship. It was times like that when he called Julie.

There were also times when he felt very alone in the world, and had considered ending it all. He was tired of the pain, sadness and loneliness, but Julie always managed to talk him out of a bad night. She reminded him of the things he had to live for, and encouraged him to put his efforts into the conservatory and farm work instead of feeling sorry for himself. He always saw a light at the end of the tunnel after talking to her - she had been responsible for keeping him alive and she didn't even know it.

Julie had been riding along in silence, lost in her own thoughts. As she thought about her relationship with Joe, she decided perhaps it was best if she let Keith in on their little "secret". She knew Joe and Keith were very good friends, and didn't want it to be a total surprise/shock to everyone when she arrived at the hospital. She was generally very good at self-composure, but with the feelings she had for Joe she wasn't sure if she could maintain that "professional" image. She feared she may completely lose it when she saw him lying in that hospital bed.

"Keith, I think there is something you should know."

Keith was lost in his own thoughts, and jumped slightly at the sound of her voice. He could feel his face flush because he felt he had been caught thinking what he had.

"Sorry, I didn't mean to startle you."

"It's okay. I was just off in my own little world."

"So was I, but I think part of that world needs to be shared before we get to the hospital. Joe speaks very highly of you, so I'm hoping I'm making the right move by telling you what I have to say."

"I have a hunch I know where this is going, and if I'm right just know it is from my own observations."

"Point taken," said Julie. "Joe and I have more than a therapist/client relationship, but I don't think anyone else knows about it. It took us a long time to get to where we're at, because he is one stubborn man."

Keith laughed, "You got that right!"

"Do you think anyone else suspects anything? You don't think Sam will be upset do you? She is a remarkable young lady, and has turned Joe's world right side up by being on the estate."

"I think Sam just wants her dad to be happy; and well. They lost a lot of time together because of her mother being such a bitch, so the past few months have been making up for it. I just hope yesterday's events didn't put an end to it all."

"Keith, do you think he's going to be okay? I'm scared to death he isn't." Tears rolled down Julie's cheeks as she thought about what might be.

"I am hoping he will be Julie. He's stubborn as a mule, and if there is anyone that can come out of something like this, it's him. I just hope whatever happened didn't wipe out the drive he has. I am still trying to deal with Chad's death; I don't think I can handle another so soon."

Keith felt tears welling up in his eyes; he wasn't one to show much emotion either, but thinking back to Chad's sudden passing left him feeling just a little overwhelmed with it all. They were entering the city limits, so he took a deep breath, wiped his eyes and tried to force a smile. "Maybe we should tell him to get his lazy ass out of bed when we get there; if he's able to hear us that should get him riled up just a little."

Julie laughed, in spite of the circumstances. She could see him giving them the finger with a comment like that. Maybe that was just what he needed; a kick in the ass, so to speak.

Keith parked the car and they walked into the hospital. They were once again lost in their own thoughts as he led the way to the ICU. Sam and Kody met them at the elevator as they had said they would. Keith had sent Sam a text when they parked; it would be easier to get back into the ICU ward if they all walked in together.

"Any change?" Keith asked after they had said their greetings and hugged one another.

"Not much in the way of his responses, but the respirator is off. The medication to keep him in a coma has been decreased gradually, so the doctor is hoping for some signs that he'll come out of whatever it is he's in." Sam was looking hopeful as she explained what they had noticed so far. "There has been some slight changes in facial movement when we've talked to him, but so far that's all we've noticed."

They had been talking while they walked into the waiting room, and Julie suddenly recalled a case theory she had read about many years before. As she explained to the others the circumstances of that particular case, they couldn't help but wonder if the same type of thing hadn't happened to Joe.

Sam walked into Joe's room and said to the nurse, "Is there any way we can speak to Dr. Walsh? A good friend of ours has some information that may help him."

The nurse had only been on shift for an hour or so, and was not willing to call the doctor at that point. Her personality seemed the complete opposite of the nurse who had been assigned to Joe when he was first admitted. Sam was feeling frustrated with the nurse's lack of cooperation, and walked over to the desk to speak with the charge nurse.

"Could I speak with you a moment please?"
"Sure,"said the charge nurse, "what can I do for you?"
"We would like to speak with Dr. Walsh. We have some information that may help him figure out what's wrong with Dad. I spoke to the nurse in with him, but she refused my request."
"I'll call him, and I'll have a word with her when she goes on her break. I have no one to cover for her right now, and I prefer not to

reprimand my nurses in front of the patients."

"Thank you," Sam said with a smile. "We're in the waiting room. If he is unable to come soon, please let me know."
"Will do Ms. Jones."

Sam went back into the waiting room and told the others of Joe's nurse and her lack of concern regarding some insight on his condition.

"If you don't mind," said Keith, "I'm going to go sit with him awhile. Call it lawyer's intuition or paranoia, but I have a bad feeling about her. I'm going to do a bit of "snooping" and see what I can find out about her."

Sam and the others were now more worried than before. First of all, who was she, and why would she refuse to call the doctor when they had what may be the missing piece to the puzzle?

Shortly after Keith left the room, the charge nurse returned with news the doctor would be with them shortly. They thanked her and waited for him, each wondering if the theory Julie had was right.

"I hear you may have some information to help," said Dr. Walsh as he walked through the door.

"Yes," replied Kody. "This is Julie; she's Joe's therapist and thinks she may know what caused him to shut down."

"Nice to meet you Dr. Walsh. I'll get right to the point, because I know you are just as anxious to get this figured out as the rest of us. A number of years ago there was a similar case where a man had suffered head injuries, and when life got to be too much for him his brain just seemed to turn off. I have been seeing Joe and helping him through the consequences of his accident for about 10 years. He has good days and bad days, but recent events may have just put him into a state of mental, emotional and psychological breakdown. It is a rare condition that most psychologists and neurologists such as yourself may only read about. I have never personally seen anything like it before, but I firmly believe there is a possibility."

"You're saying he has simply turned off the world?" Dr. Walsh had never encountered anything quite so bizarre in his entire medical career, but he was not so closed minded that he didn't think it was possible. He had heard of strange things happening, but they always seemed to happen to other people.

"Well Julie, you may be onto something. What do you propose we do to see if your theory is right? I'm willing to work with you on this, but I must add that I am still his doctor and I will pull rank if necessary."

"We understand that, but we have to try. As crazy as it seems, we honestly think the only thing that may bring him around is an alpaca."

"A WHAT?" Dr. Walsh was more bewildered than surprised with what they were proposing.

Kody stepped in and said, "Your hospital supports animal therapy, does it not?"

"Yes, it does - but dogs are the usual animal of choice. But an alpaca? Where in the world are we supposed to get one of those?"

"He raises them. They have been his therapy for many years. It was the alpacas that gave him some purpose while he was recovering from the accident; they don't demand anything from him and he loves to sit with them. We can have his favorite one brought in if you'll allow it. We're at wits end Dr. Walsh - we're willing to try anything right now. Please?" It was Sam who spoke. "We're not ready to give up on him yet, no matter what. I know it has only been 24 hours, but it seems like an eternity to us."

"Alright, you have my support. There are some procedures the animals must go through before entering the hospital though. I'll send in our Animal Therapy Coordinator and she can make the arrangements. In the meantime, I will continue to monitor him and discontinue the medication I have him on. Hopefully he will start to come around. If he is in pain, it's important we know so we can help with that. I must admit, when I came to work I did not think I would be having a conversation even remotely close to the one we just had. It's good when family members make me think outside the box once in awhile." He smiled and walked out the door.

Keith returned shortly after the doctor left. "The charge nurse sent in another nurse. I think I figured out who the other one is. I have asked for her to be assigned to another patient, just for safety's sake."

Sam felt her heart skip a beat. "Who the hell is she?"

"She is a very good friend of your mom's. I did a little prying; casual conversation you know. She has been led to believe Joe has been a deadbeat dad all these years, and a verbally abusive husband. I think she has been so caught up in the lies she has been told she was willing to risk her career and her freedom just to help Sally get "revenge". She has agreed to meet with me at the end of her shift; she will be set straight once and for all."

"Shit! Joe had better wake up soon if he knows what's good for him," said Kody. "This does not seem like a good place to be. It could be hazardous to his health."

CHAPTER TEN

Sam was really beginning to despise her mother more with each passing minute. Who else had she conned into believing Joe was an unfit husband and uncaring father? She could feel her stress levels multiplying quickly. Luckily, her thoughts were interrupted by the Animal Therapy Coordinator.

"Good afternoon everyone. My name is Rachel and I am the Animal Therapy Coordinator. Dr. Walsh tells me you have some thought of your own in terms of a therapeutic animal."

"Yes, we do," replied Julie. "I am Joe's psychologist and friend, and I firmly believe allowing his favourite alpaca to visit him will do wonders. They have been his therapy for many years, and I think he needs to know they still need him as much as he needs them. I know you usually work with dogs, but we would really like the chance to bring one in."

"Well, I do know there are some that go to schools in other parts of the country, but we have never had one here. I don't imagine the risk of them biting anyone is very high?"
"No," Kody laughed. "Even the spit factor will be minimal here. What do we have to do to get it ready?"
"Give it a bath, make sure it isn't going to make a mess on the floor and keep it restrained at all times. I'm almost done for the day, but you can bring it in tomorrow morning sometime. I want to be here for this!"

"Thank you very much Rachel! You won't be disappointed."

After Rachel left the room, Sam called Parker.

"You want me to do what?!" He couldn't believe his ears. "Have you lost your mind?"
"Not at all Parker. In fact, this feels more right than anything has in a long time. Please help us out on this one. Kody will give you some instructions and let you know where everything is for transport. Oh, and Parker - quit laughing!"

Parker couldn't help himself. He was beside himself and had tears rolling down his cheeks. He knew Sam had some crazy ideas sometimes, but this took the cake. But, being the friend that he was, he agreed to do as she asked. He listened to Kody and made a list of things he had to do. As much as he thought Sam had completely lost her marbles, he couldn't help but love her. He pushed some thoughts from his mind and went to the barn to get Joe's favourite girl ready.

It had been decided Parker and Simon would make the trip the next day, after the morning chores were done. Parker was still laughing and shaking his head when he got to the barn to get Lulu ready. There wasn't much to do besides adjust the halter and make sure she wasn't full of hay or other bits of stuff. He decided blowing her off in the morning would make more sense, as she would be with the rest of the girls until it was time to leave. He went into the office and retrieved her vaccination record, just in case Rachel wanted to see them.

The next morning, Parker and Simon did the chores a little earlier than they had been told to, simply because it was a two hour drive to the hospital. Parker haltered Lulu and blew her off; something she was quite used to. Joe always paid special attention to her, and she was the one that he took to shows. She was also the one who was most accustomed to riding in the van, as that was how she usually travelled.

It had been decided that Parker should take Lulu to his house first so she could have some hay, water and relieve herself. Since it was going to be very unfamiliar territory, he had put a small scoop of alpaca beans in a Ziploc bag. Putting the beans on his lawn would encourage her to "go", and he had every intention of leaving them there. He would rake them up in the spring and add them to his small garden plot.

Parker drove into his driveway, and he and Simon helped Lulu out of the van. She had been cushed for the entire drive, and they thought her legs must be stiff by then. As he walked her through the gate into the backyard, Parker noticed his neighbours peeking through their window. He smiled and waved, and within minutes they had ventured out to get a closer look. It didn't take long before there were several other passersby taking a look at the strange animal in his backyard.

After Lulu was fed, watered and had her bathroom break, Parker called Sam to see if they were ready for her. Sam said they would be in about a half hour, but that he could leave soon if he wished. It would take several minutes to get the little crowd that had gathered to disperse so they could put her back in the van. Parker assured them he would be back with her in a couple hours or so, and that they could have another visit with her then. Lulu had become an instant attraction, and Parker found himself quite at ease talking about her and alpacas in general. He had been educated in their many traits and aspects before Christmas during the Open House at the estate.

When they arrived at the hospital, Rachel met them at the pedway entrance. She was worried Lulu would make a mess on the floor, but Parker and Simon assured her she would be fine. As they walked through the hospital and into the elevator, they had strange looks from almost everyone they saw. Those who just smiled knew what that strange animal was, and they understood its purpose in the hospital.

Lulu was humming softly as she walked beside Parker; a sign she was feeling a little stressed with all of the activity and strange sounds. The people themselves didn't bother her much, but the strange smells and beeps of monitors and alarm bells were causing her some anxiety.

They knew this was a make or break visit, and they didn't have much time. Sam took over when they got to the door of Joe's room, and her and Kody walked Lulu into the room and closed the door. The nurse on duty had been on the night Joe was brought in, and had been informed of the special visitor. She had never seen a real alpaca before, so was full of questions. As the three of them talked and Lulu hummed, Joe's blood pressure dropped by a few points. It had been just above normal since his arrival, but dropped for the first time.

Sam was very excited; she knew he could hear Lulu. He was always more relaxed when he was with the alpacas. The nurse had Dr. Walsh paged, and he arrived within minutes. He had already made his rounds and had not been too happy with Joe's condition, which had remained virtually unchanged since the previous evening. He knew the visit was scheduled for that morning, so he took his time in the unit so he could see for himself if the animal made any difference.

"Unbelievable! I honestly didn't think this would work," he said as he watched the monitors. "I think I have found a new appreciation for the work these animals do. If I hadn't just been in here and worried about his indifference to anything we've tried, I would have thought you were pulling my leg. Joe, can you hear me? You have a special visitor. She would like you to wake up and say hello."

Dr. Walsh and the others watched for a response. Lulu continued to hum softly beside the bed. She seemed to recognize Joe, but couldn't quite grasp why he wasn't talking to her like he always did. After what seemed like an eternity, Joe whispered "Hi Lulu! Where is everyone else? I'll feed you in a minute."

"Dad! Dad, can you hear me?" Sam tried hard to contain her excitement, and tried to keep her voice down, but felt she wasn't being very quiet.

Joe's eyes slowly opened and he looked at them with an expression of both confusion and wonder. He didn't remember what had happened, and couldn't quite figure out why Lulu was beside his bed. As everything began to come into focus he asked, "what the hell happened to me, and why is Lulu here?"

Dr. Walsh introduced himself and briefly filled Joe in on the events of the last couple of days. He explained the surgery and the coma, and the lack of response to anything they tried to wake him up. "I must say Joe, I am both shocked and amazed that this animal did what the medical profession and all its knowledge couldn't do. I am truly humbled by this experience. It just goes to show that there are other forces at work here. I'm not talking about God either. The power this animal has is simply amazing." This time it was the doctor who got teary-eyed, and he fought them as hard as he could. "Welcome back Joe. I'll be back this evening to see how you're doing."

Sam, Kody and the nurse were also teary-eyed. This had been nothing short of a miracle in their eyes. A miracle that Joe was not only awake, but that he also seemed to have no lapse in his memory prior to passing out. It was one for the record books, that was for sure.

"Well Dad, I'm afraid it's time to take Lulu home. Parker is waiting for her. I'll send Julie and Keith in. Jason and Emily will be by in a little while to see you. I love you."

"Julie's here? Why?" Joe was upset that they called her; he didn't want her to see him like that.

"Easy Joe," said Kody. "If it hadn't been for her, we wouldn't have thought about bringing Lulu. It helps to have a trained psychologist on board. She was going on a whim when she suggested Lulu; and it worked. Don't be angry with Sam or anyone else."

Joe closed his eyes, and they all thought he was gone again. "Fine, have it your way," he said after a moment. Sighs of relief filled the room, and Sam and Kody led Lulu out the door, but not until Joe was able to stroke her neck for a minute.

Keith and Julie were waiting outside the door with Simon and Parker. They hugged Sam and Kody and then Julie went in to see Joe alone for a moment. It had been decided she would ride back with Parker, Simon and Lulu as Keith had some business to take care of in the city.

"I hear you're responsible for this," Joe said as Julie walked through the door.

Her heart sank, as she thought he meant the reason he was in the hospital. She didn't know what to say, but was quickly reassured when he said, "they tell me you were the one who suggested Lulu be brought in. Thank you Julie!"

She went to his side and took his hand, "I couldn't imagine you not being around. We had to try something. Now, would you care to tell me what has been going on with you?"

Out in the waiting room Lulu was getting all sorts of attention from both family members of patients and staff alike. Rachel had returned and pulled Sam aside. "Is there any possible way we can make her a regular visitor to the hospital? I think she would be great in the Children's Ward. Give it some thought and let me know. She has most definitely earned her stripes today."

Getting Lulu out of the hospital was more difficult than bringing her in had been. Word had spread about the strange animal and they were surrounded by people every step of the way, right out to the van. Lulu was becoming very stressed with all of the activity, and getting her to a quiet backyard was what they wanted to do. They knew there would be more people showing up as soon as they drove in, but the noise level would be nowhere near what the hospital had been.

CHAPTER ELEVEN

With Lulu tucked safely back in the barn with the rest of the girls, Parker drove Julie back to her house. The ride from the city had been filled with conversation about the day's events, and what a hit Lulu had been. Julie suggested Parker should seriously consider doing what he enjoyed, as she could clearly see he thoroughly enjoyed working with the alpacas.

The conversation left the wheels turning as he drove back to the estate. He did enjoy the fresh air, the quiet of the estate and the alpacas. Perhaps it was time he took another look at his life, and what he wanted from it. He recalled the awe he felt when he saw the cria being born, and how much he didn't want to go back to the city. He had some decisions to make, and he wanted Sam's input.

Sam had always told him he looked out of place in the city, and that his four wheel drive had country boy written all over it. He always argued the point with her and said he couldn't leave the city because it was where he should be. Now he was questioning his own decisions, and was beginning to think that perhaps Sam had been right all along. He wanted to make sure he was ready for the "I told you so" speech she was sure to give him.

They were incompatible as a couple, but did great together when it came to matters of the heart. He missed Sam and the fun they had together, but knew she would always be there for him as a friend. He was missing the "benefits" part of their friendship - and he had a feeling he may never get that benefit again.

He had decided to sleep on the sofa and let Simon have the spare room. He had contemplated claiming Sam's king size bed, but decided it was best if he stayed out of her room. He couldn't bear the thought of her sleeping there with Kody and not him. Some things were just hard to let go of, no matter how hard he tried.

CHAPTER TWELVE

With Joe awake and seeming to be out of the woods, everyone relaxed. Kody decided it was alright for him to go back to work; rather Joe decided for him. The hardware store could function without him there, he argued, but Joe would have none of that. Rather than piss Joe off completely, Kody agreed and said his goodbye's to Sam.

After Kody left, Sam felt she had to do something or she feared she would go just as insane as her mother was. She was a writer, after all!

She walked down to the Gift Shop in the hospital and bought a notebook. Sure she had her phone, but she needed to see the words on paper. She had written thousands of articles over the years, and several white papers but she wanted something more. Writing was a good way for her to relax, and carrying a notebook around was much easier than a tote full of material or yarn (she loved to quilt and to crochet). She had a storyline in mind, and decided just to see where it would take her.

Joe was still going to be in ICU for at least another day and she wanted to be close without being in the way. She went to the family waiting room, sat in one of the big armchairs, and started to write:

Penny looked across the field and still couldn't believe it was all hers.

She could see two horses in the distance and could hear the frogs in the pond. There were geese flying overhead, a sure sign spring must be there to stay.

She had finally secured a quarter of land she would soon be able to call home. It was just land with a well and power, but no septic system. That would all have to be put in, but she would worry about that later. First, she had to plan it all out and budget accordingly. It was just her, so she didn't need much to begin with. As she sat in her truck bed she made a list of things she had to do. As much as she wanted to build her barn and paddocks, she knew the cabin would have to come first.

Now was the perfect time to start; the snow was gone and the summer heat hadn't set in yet. She was fairly handy with tools and knew how to read a tape measure. All she really needed at this point was a roof over her head. She wanted a bigger house, but that would come later. her cabin could serve as the guest house down the road.

As she drew out her plans and made a list of building materials she would need, she heard an approaching vehicle. She hadn't told anyone about this place; she needed a retreat and this was going to be it. She needed a place to escape from the outside world; a place where she could be creative without limitations.

Penny turned her head as the vehicle came to a stop several yards from hers. What she saw get out of the truck was some of the best eye candy she had seen in quite some time. He was tall, lean and from what she could see, filled out his Wranglers in all the right places. She wondered who he was, and had a feeling she was about to find out.

"Howdy Ma'am" he said as he tipped his black cowboy hat. "I saw you drive by awhile ago; just being neighbourly and making sure no one is vandalizing the place.
"Well, that is awfully kind of you, but why would I want to vandalize my own place?"
"You bought it?" He seemed a little taken aback; perhaps he was expecting someone different. "Pleased to meet you" he said as he extended his hand to hers. "I'm Ben. I live down the road; those are

my horses over there," and he pointed across the field.

"Nice to meet you too. I'm Penny." She reached out and shook his hand. His touch sent tingles down her spine; a feeling she wasn't accustomed to.

Never in a million years did she expect to have a neighbour who looked that good. He had to be married; the hot ones usually were. She thought for a moment about how she could find out without seeming too nosy.

"Which horse is yours and which one is your wife's?"
"Um, they're both mine. No wife, just me and my animals."
"I was going to say she was one lucky lady, but I see there's no need."

Sam really liked where the story was going. She flipped to the back of her notebook and started to outline the chapters. She knew an outline before she started would have been more pleasing to her English teacher, but over the years she had found a system that worked for her. Fiction was a new experience for her, but the basic principles were the same. Outline; write; edit; write; edit; repeat; submit. She had done part of it ass-backwards, but there were no novel police handing out tickets, so she just did it her way.

When she checked the time she realized she had been there for over an hour. She was sure Joe would be wondering where she was, so she packed up her notebook and went to his room. She found him sitting up and chatting it up with the nurse, who was checking the drainage tube in his head.

"Do I really need to have this thing hooked up to me?" he asked, referring to the catheter.
"Yes you do. It's better if we leave it until after your surgery to close everything up. Unless of course you would like us to put another in while you're awake?"
"Ummm...no thanks! Been there, done that! I'll suffer and you can have it your way."

Sam could tell he was feeling better, because he was being his smart-assed self.

"Hi Dad! How are you feeling?" she asked as she gave him a hug.

"I'd feel a lot better if I could pee the right way."

"Now Joe," the nurse said, "didn't we just have that conversation? Or are you trying to get some sympathy from your daughter?"

Joe looked at Sam, smiled and nodded toward the nurse, "Can't pull the wool over her eyes."

Sam laughed then asked the nurse, "When does he go back into surgery?"

"We have a CT scheduled in an hour, and the doctor will decide after he sees the results. It could be later today or first thing in the morning. Dr. Walsh wants to get him patched up so he can kick him out. He really is becoming a pain in the butt." As she made the last comment, she winked at Joe as he stuck his tongue out at her.

"See what I have to put up with Sam?"

"Someone has to keep you in line Dad. They're probably easier on you than we are anyway."

Joe thought for a minute, then said, "Good point." Then he changed the subject, "How did Lulu manage the trip? Is she settled back in?"

"Lulu is just fine Dad. Parker said she settled right back in as soon as he put her in the barn. He sure seems to have a way with her. Maybe you could teach him a thing or two about them before he leaves."

"I don't think there's much to teach; he jumped right in when I need help before Christmas. He might just be a natural."

Sam thought so too, and she was going to have a talk with Parker when she got home. She had a feeling an opportunity may have just opened up for him; it was up to him to act on it.

CHAPTER THIRTEEN

Joe's CT scan was over and done, and they anxiously awaited results. Jason had left work early (he too went back to work the previous day when he learned Joe would be fine) so he could be there with Sam just in case things didn't look so good on screen.

They hadn't really talked about the events in the courtroom since Joe woke up, and Sam was afraid to bring up the subject. She was afraid it would cause undue stress for Joe, and didn't want to see him in another coma. She knew the issue would have to be discussed sooner or later, as there was still the matter of the divorce. Her hesitations and reservations about the subject matter were worrying her for nothing, because he was the first to bring it up.

"Has anyone heard from Sally since she was hauled away by security?"
"She had the hospital call Emily, Uncle Joe," replied Jason. "I'm not sure why, but I'm sure Emily will tell us when she gets here."
"She has a way with Sally, that's for sure. I'm not sure if that's a good thing or a bad thing, but either way it is what it is. Where's Keith? I have some questions for him regarding the divorce now that she's in a psyche ward."

"He said he'd come see you later, but we told him you might be going back into surgery tonight. He said to call him if you're not and he'll come visit. If you do go in, he'll wait until you're back in your bed and alert." Sam chose her words carefully, as Keith had said a few other things as well. She decided to stop at that and let the two of them discuss the other matters when the time came.

"I don't think she realizes she isn't going to come out as far ahead as she thinks she is. She knows what my payout was years ago, and I think she still believes there is that much still available. With her getting over a quarter of a million dollars of it over the last 10 years, there isn't much to work with anymore. Boy, is she going to be pissed when she finds out! She's going to be even more pissed when her money from me gets based on my income, not what I was giving her before. I don't think she'll be filing any hardship claims either."

Joe thought for a moment, then continued on. "The income I receive is based on the interest from my insurance, which is less than 100k now. The estate is its own entity, which means I have little power or control over the amount of dollars going in or out. Keith has been given the power to manage the financial end of it, as Chad wanted someone not in the immediate family to have an interest in it as well. It's a complicated system, but it works for the most part. Less chance of family members being screwed over. I'll have to get Keith to explain it all to you, since the system will be 100% yours one day."

Sam wasn't sure what to think. She hadn't really questioned the financial aspect of the estate before; she just knew it was all being taken care of. She suspected Joe hadn't planned on saying anything to her, but given the recent events he must have felt she should at least be somewhat in the loop. From what she could see, the only expenses the estate had were the utilities, fuel and insurance. Oh, and the fees for Keith. She didn't know how much he was earning each month just from the estate alone, but at that point, she didn't really want to. Sam knew it couldn't be cheap to run such an operation as Joe had been managing, and she was glad there was someone trustworthy on their side.

As Sam opened her mouth to ask a question about the estate, Dr. Walsh walked in.

"Good afternoon everyone! Joe, it's good to see you still with us. I'm afraid I have some bad news for you. I am not going to stitch you back up just yet, because something still doesn't look right. I have scheduled a few more tests, in hopes of ruling out my suspicions. I'm going to level with you Joe; it doesn't look promising. I am really hoping I'm wrong on this one, but I think we're dealing with a brain tumour. I've spoken with an oncologist and we've reviewed the CTs together; not looking good at all."

The room suddenly got very quiet, and Sam started to cry. "Are you sure?"

"Not 100% yet Ms. Jones, but the signs, symptoms and seizures all lead to a growth that is causing problems very quickly in the brain. We're going to do whatever we can, but I have to be honest with you; it might not be enough at this stage of the game. I have some tests scheduled for tomorrow. Joe, the nurse will take you down in the morning. I'm truly sorry guys; I thought it was all going to be okay too."

Dr. Walsh left the room, and Joe laid back on the bed. "I was afraid of this. Jason, call Keith. Tell him to get his ass over here as soon as he can; and bring his laptop up."

CHAPTER FOURTEEN

The next day was a blur for Sam and the others. There were blood tests, more scans, reaction time tests and cognitive thinking tests. One of the biggest challenges was the memory testing. Some of the questions brought quick responses from Joe, while others caused him mild anxiety when he struggled to remember.

Sam had called Kody the evening before, and he made the trip to be there for her and Joe. It had been decided that Julie was not to be told until all of the results had come back. Even Parker and Simon had only been told they'd be needed for at least another few days. Simon traveled to the city with Kody to get his own vehicle. He had made the trip out with Parker but needed to be back at work the following week.

As Sam went from test to test with Joe, she spent several hours in waiting rooms. She wrote in her notebook to pass the time and to take her mind off of the inevitable. She was very afraid of what was to be, and even more afraid of the unknown. She didn't want to think about it, but the thoughts kept creeping back into her head.

Keith had shown her and Jason the estate records, both ownership and financial. Although Sam had been named heir, it wasn't without some conditions that had to be met in order for the estate to continue to remain as functional as it was. Sam had a lot to learn over the next few weeks, and she wasn't sure she could do it alone. She was feeling overwhelmed, but forced herself to calm down and take it all in stride. Nothing they did was going to change the test results; it was something they had to deal with no matter how difficult it was.

By the end of the day, Joe was exhausted. The doctor prescribed him some medication so he would sleep; it would also give the rest of them some time to go back to Jason's and relax. They knew who his nurse was going to be at shift change, so they had nothing to worry about. The friend of Sally's who had been his nurse a couple days before had been given a temporary leave of absence and security were asked to escort her to the door should she return at any time during the course of Joe's stay.

Some of Jason and Emily's staff had been busy during the day as well, and it had nothing to do with the business. They had taken the day to cook a few meals, bake some squares and stock Jason's fridge with drinks; both alcoholic and nonalcoholic. It was the type of thing they had been doing since the beginning, no matter who was in need of some help. Chad had not only instilled some real values in his own family, those same values were instilled in his long-time employees as well. Whenever someone in the company was ill or in need of assistance in some way, Chad made sure they were taken care of. It was something that continued on even after his death. Jason was forever grateful to his dad for showing others it was okay to care; that it was okay to help and expect nothing in return. He had done his fair share of shoveling snow, cutting lawns and helping members of their staff when they had a personal crisis.

Jason recalled the hours they had spent at Leon's when he had been hurt in an automobile accident a few years before. Chad insisted the yard maintenance be done, and personally took Leon to physio and doctor's appointments. The accident hadn't even happened during work hours or with a company vehicle; it had been the result of a drunk driver while Leon was returning from a weekend at the lake. It was during the days that Jason helped his dad do unpaid work that he learned the most.

"Jason, where do you want me to put this?"

He was brought back to reality when Sam spoke as she held up a huge basket of food. "Sorry Sam...ummm, how about on the dining room table."

A stack of Royal Chinet plates had been left on the counter, which they all appreciated. That meant there were that many less dishes to contend with after they ate. Real food had been somewhat of a rarity the last couple of days, so being fed things like meatloaf, perogies, cabbage rolls, ham and a variety of salads was a welcome change. The dessert tray was filled with brownies, coconut squares, peanut butter bars and even some homemade doughnuts.

Even though they didn't feel hungry when they started, they each ate more than they thought they would. There had been a couple of bottles of wine opened as well, so they each poured a glass. It had been a very long couple of days (had it only been a couple of days?), and they welcomed the chance to relax and talk.

The chatter varied from the estate to Joe to the court appearance that seemed to trigger it all. They now knew it was simply coincidence, but felt the stress may have sped up the process just a little. Perhaps it was better that way, as Joe was with loved ones and able to get the immediate care he needed. Keith shuddered at the thought of someone finding Joe out in the barn or in his bed. It had all played out to his (Joe's) advantage; he may have suffered for several hours had he been alone when it happened.

Jason started to clear the table when everyone was finished with their meal and Sam got up to help. "What am I going to do Jason? I can't bear the thought of losing him now. I think it's much worse knowing what the eventual outcome is going to be."

"I disagree Sam. At least this time we'll get to say goodbye." He had tears in his eyes as he painfully recalled the day he found out Chad had suffered a massive heart attack and died. Chad had been out on the golf course and took a swing, walked five steps and dropped to the ground. He was pronounced dead on arrival at the hospital, but only because they had kept his blood flowing by trying to resuscitate him. It had been very devastating to all, and had put up walls between Jason, Emily and Sam. Jason and Emily had been bitter about the estate going to Sam, but as the weeks went on and they learned more about it, the bitterness dissipated.

Sam too thought back to the day she heard about Uncle Chad and said, "Yes, you are right in that regard. I just don't want him to suffer for months on end; that's going to be the hardest part."

"Dad was just going to play one round; told me he'd call when he was done and we'd go for a coffee. When my phone rang I thought it was him...it wasn't. It was the police calling to tell me the bad news. I thought they had made a mistake, and told them so. They told me if I had any doubts then I should go to the hospital morgue and identify the body. They were very kind and offered help, but it was too late for that."

It had been the first time since Chad's death that Sam and Jason had actually talked about that day. The days after he died had been filled with many tears, disbelief, anger and grief. That was all on top of the process of the funeral arrangements, condolences from current and past customers, visits from friends and family and just getting through each day knowing he wasn't ever going to walk through the door again.

Sam had her friends, and that was where she had spent most of her time for the first few weeks after his death. They made sure she ate, and did what they could to get her to think of the good times her and Uncle Chad had. Her and Jason had never really had an opportunity to talk, and the Reading of the Will forced them apart. It hadn't been intentional, but the loss was still so new they assumed she had put him up to it. Jason admitted to feeling like a real tool when Keith sat him and Emily down and explained the situation to them. Emily refused to be the first one to apologize, and Jason had good intentions, but never actually picked up the phone to call her.

As they talked about the last few months, they agreed Christmas had been the hardest. For Sam Christmas had been bittersweet, because she had Joe in her life again but Uncle Chad was gone. A perfect Christmas would have been having them both there. She didn't want to think about what the next Christmas might be like.

"Anyone for a refill?" asked Kody as he walked into the kitchen with a bottle of wine in each hand (one red, one white).

"Yes please," they both said at the same time, then laughed.

Kody filled their glasses and went into the living room, where the others had settled.

"I guess I should go out and entertain my guests. After you Sam." They joined the others and spent the next two or three hours reminiscing about the past and wondering what the future held for the family.

CHAPTER FIFTEEN

Sam, Jason and Kody arrived at the hospital the next morning by 8. As they walked into the ICU ward, the charge nurse pulled them aside.

"I'm afraid we had a bit of a situation here earlier. Joe is resting now, but he did have a seizure that was quite serious. Dr. Evans from Oncology, and Dr. Walsh will be in to speak with you shortly. They asked me to page them as soon as you got here."

The three of them looked at one another, and their hearts felt heavy. It appeared they may not have as much time as they had first thought; if only there was something that could be done.

A few minutes later, the doctors walked into the family room together and sat down with them. Dr. Walsh started, "We know you came here this morning full of hope, but as you've been told, this is progressing rapidly. The seizure this morning is a telltale sign of damage being done in his brain at an alarming rate. We're going to try to slow it down, but there are no guarantees."

Dr. Evans then spoke. "I would like to start an aggressive chemotherapy treatment, but I'm afraid the side effects may make him very ill. We have to evaluate the quality of life he'll have in either scenario - with treatment or without treatment. I generally advise my patients and their families to opt for treatment, but there are occasionally cases where keeping the patient comfortable is the best we can do. My analysis of all of the testing we have done says this may be one of those cases."

Sam couldn't believe her ears. Had they already given up on him? Or was it really as serious as they said?

"I'm having a very hard time believing it is progressing so quickly," she said through tears. "Why wasn't it found before? How could it not be there one day and causing seizures the next? Forgive me, but I just can't fathom anything spreading that fast inside a human body."

"I know it's hard to believe Sam," said Dr. Walsh. "We don't come across cases like this very often; in fact, this is maybe the third in as many decades that we have personally encountered. The research in the last decade has made a big difference in survival rates; or perhaps I should say the 'prolonged life' rates. We are going to do what we can, but we want you to know his chances are grim. When he wakes up I think it would be a good idea for us to explain it to him as well. We do not try to play God around here; quality of life is number one. If he has a good month or two doing the things he enjoys, that is far better than several months or even years of laying in bed unable to do much for himself. We as doctors want to try the medicines and surgeries to fix him, but as human beings we value each individual as a person with hopes, dreams and feelings. Our patients are not just numbers; they are real people with real life-threatening conditions. We urge you to make some final arrangements with him if it hasn't been done yet, before he can no longer function mentally."

"We are very sorry we couldn't bring you better news folks," said the oncologist, "but this is one of those situations where sugar coating could leave many people unprepared. We'll have the nurse page us when he wakes up. After we talk to him we'll figure out a treatment plan; or a get-through-the-next-few-weeks plan. He will be the one to decide what happens. We urge you to respect his wishes, no matter how selfish they may seem."

The doctors left the room and the three of them sat completely still, as if frozen to their spots. Several minutes went by, and tears streamed down each of their faces. After a little while Sam stood up and left the room. Kody stood to go with her, but Jason stopped him.

"Let her go Kody. She needs to be alone for a bit. I'm sure she'll head straight to his room. She needs to face this head on. He had so much planned for her, and knowing him he'll tough it out until she knows what he expects. She's stronger than you think she is Kody; don't smother her or you'll lose her. Is that what you want?"

Kody sat back down, even though he hated being told to do so. He had gotten along with Jason so far, but being stepped on like that did not sit well with him. He was not used to being told to stay put, and with all of the stress of recent days he wanted nothing more than to hit something or someone.

Jason recognized the look in Kody's eyes and vowed he would kick his ass if he ever so much as attempted to lay a hand on anyone in his family, especially Sam. He felt Kody was hiding a part of his past, but had nothing to go on but a feeling. He made a note to do a little searching on his own, then dialed Keith's number.

An hour after Sam had left the waiting room, Keith met her in Joe's room. He then sent Jason a text telling him to meet them, and to send Kody for coffee. As helpful as Kody had been through all of what had happened, this was a matter for family only.

"Kody, you look like you could use some fresh air. Could you please go across the street and get us all some coffee and doughnuts?" Jason handed Kody a $20 bill "My treat."

After Kody left the ICU, Jason went to the desk and told the nurse to send him to Joe's room when he returned. Whatever Keith had to say needed to be said quickly. There was something about Kody that suddenly was rubbing him the wrong way, and he wasn't quite sure what it was.

Joe was awake when Jason entered his room, and Keith got right to the point. "Joe has decided to rewrite his Will, and he would like you to be an executor. He has made some changes to it so it is now as current as it can be. It's one of those things that we put off for various reasons, and your dad was still an executor. The deceased do not make valid executors and the courts will eat up any assets in cases like that. Do you feel comfortable with the delegation Jason?"

"Yes, I will do whatever Uncle Joe asks of me." he looked over at Joe and Sam and smiled. "We're in it for the long haul, aren't we?"

"Damn rights we are!" stated Joe. "I don't want anyone pussy footin' around me. There's work to be done."

A few minutes later Kody returned with coffee and doughnuts for everyone. The coffee hit the spot, and Joe started talking about the upcoming cria season. He looked over at Sam and said, "You might want to be writing some of this stuff down. You and your new business partner are going to need it."

Sam gave him a "what the heck are you talking about?" look, but then realized what he was getting at. She had a feeling Kody was going to be just a tad angry over what was to come, but it wasn't for him to decide.

The doctors entered the room and explained the options to Joe. Sam had already filled him in on what they had said to her earlier, and he was surprisingly calm about it all. When Dr. Walsh voiced his concern over the indifference Joe seemed to be displaying, Joe said, "I have been near death once before, and recovery hurt like hell. I was afraid of dying; afraid of never knowing my little girl. I'm not afraid anymore, because I have been through hell on earth. My heaven on earth is Sam, and now that I know she is the person I dreamed she would be, I can live out the rest of my days by her side. I want to 'live' my last days, not spend them waiting for death. Do what you can to keep me from seizing every few hours and the rest will take care of itself. I want to go home so I can enjoy the time I have left. The last place I want to be is in here hooked up to all this crap; just so I can see if my heart is still beating."

"Your wish is our command Joe. We will send you to your local hospital with a list of meds. If you can tolerate them for 48 hours with minimal episodes (none is a better number), you can go home and go about your daily routine as much as possible. If you need assistance, please call the Home Care Office and they will help you. We'll call for an ambulance to do the transfer, but we do want to see you back here in two weeks time. We will do another assessment and see if we need to make any adjustments."

"He's yours in 48 hours, if he behaves." said Dr. Evans. If he doesn't, you can always ship him back to us."

With that the duo walked out the door, and there were little cheers all around. It had turned out to be a good day after all; even with the news weighing heavily on their shoulders.

CHAPTER SIXTEEN

With Joe closer to home, Sam was finally able to sleep in her own bed. It was after midnight when she unlocked the door and went inside, expecting everyone to be asleep. She was hoping she could just sneak in unseen and go to bed, but Parker was on the sofa and heard her come in.

"Well, well...look who finally decided to come home," he teased. "How are you Sam?"
"Tired. Smartass! What are you still doing awake? Have you been sleeping on the sofa all week?"
"Couldn't sleep, and yes I have. Simon has the spare bed, and I didn't want to mess yours up."
"Well, it's no wonder you couldn't sleep. It's not the most comfortable piece of furniture I own."
"It's just fine; was just thinking, that's all."
Sam couldn't resist, "So that's why I smelled smoke when I walked in."

The next thing she knew she had a cushion flying at her, and she ducked just in time as it sailed past her head. She put her bag and purse down, picked up the cushion and threw it back, hitting him on the shoulder. He didn't have as much room to move as she did, since he was in a semi-sitting position.

Parker wanted nothing more at that moment than to take her in his arms and hold her. He had been doing a lot of thinking since his trip with Lulu, and wanted Sam's opinion. His thoughts often strayed away from the alpacas and into Sam's bedroom, and that wasn't making it any easier for him to stay focussed.

"I'm going upstairs to shower. Could you please open a bottle of wine? I am ready for a nightcap."
"Sure thing Sam. Red or white?"
"White please. Red makes me frisky. Shit, maybe I shouldn't have told you that." She walked away before he could reply, and it was just as well. There was no way he could have stood up without her noticing the boner he was sporting, especially since he was just in his boxers.

He watched her walk down the hall, and as she did she took out her ponytail and let her hair fall on her shoulders and part way down her back. It took every ounce of willpower not to follow her and have his way with her. Dammit, why did she have to fall for Kody? He knew she'd never sleep with him as long as she was in a relationship. He could see this turning into a long night, and not in a bad way. Well, bad for him, because he'd be taking care of his problem on his own.

He went into the kitchen and chose a bottle of white wine (even though he was very tempted to pick red). He went to the China Cabinet and got two wine glasses, found the corkscrew in a drawer and set everything on the coffee table. He fluffed up his pillow and put one at the other end of the sofa for Sam. He knew she had a rough week, so wanted to pamper her just a little; as much as he dared anyway.

Sam stood in the shower and let the hot water spray over her. She had been hoping for no one to be awake when she walked in the door, but maybe it wasn't a bad thing that it was Parker who was up. She had been meaning to talk to him anyway; she just hoped that they could stay at talking. As she lathered up the bath sponge and soaped herself up, she was beginning to feel more relaxed; maybe even a little horny. She let her hands do the walking and rubbed the body wash on her breasts, squeezing them a little more than she intended to. She wasn't quite sure how she was going to get through the next hour or two with Parker; perhaps she should be using cold water in the shower instead of hot.

After her shower she went back downstairs wrapped in only a towel. She had combed her hair and was letting it air dry. She usually put it in a braid or ponytail, but she would be going to bed soon so there was no need.

"Thank you," she said as Parker handed her the glass of wine. "I think I could drink the whole bottle tonight, but please make sure I don't. I will be heading back to the hospital in the morning. I really don't want to show up there hungover."

"I won't. See. I'm helping you drink it. How are you holding up Sam?"

"I'll be okay. I'm possibly going to have a new business partner, but before that happens I have to learn all there is to know about the alpaca side of this place. Dad has me working on a list already; I'll be adding to it as the days go on."

"Business partner? Anyone I know?" Parker was not looking forward to the answer, as he thought for sure it must be Kody. Much to his surprise, Sam did not mention Kody's name at all. In fact, she hadn't mentioned any name. All she said was she had a feeling the new partner would be thrilled and it was an opportunity they would hopefully jump at. That had him even more confused, but he decided to just be there for her no matter what.

"Where's Kody tonight?" he questioned. He had expected Sam to have Kody with her when she got home.

"I sent him home. I really just want quiet tonight; no demands, no constant chatter about the hardware store and definitely no talk about anything serious. He's been great through all of this, but I can't help but feel something's just not right. I might just be tired and my mind could be playing tricks on me, but I think there's a darker side to him than anyone cares to let on. If I'm wrong, I'll be the first to admit it."

"No talk about anything serious, eh Sam? That sounds pretty serious to me." Parker was concerned, and decided at that moment that he would do whatever it took to protect her. "You really shouldn't have come down here in that towel. I'd hate for it to fall off and give you a chill."

Sam laughed. "If it falls off it's only because you helped it."

He started to stand up, and she thought he was taking her last comment as a challenge, but he went into the kitchen instead. She could hear the fridge door open and close, and then the pantry door. A few minutes later he emerged with a plate of snacks for them; something he had prepared earlier in the day when she said she was going to be home that night.

"Parker, you're such a sweetheart. You do think of everything, don't you?"
"I wasn't sure if you'd be hungry, so I decided to make something that could be eaten tonight or would keep until tomorrow." He knew it was the little things that made a difference to her; he had known her a long time and had seen her go through both good and bad. He only hoped it would be enough to make her see he still deeply cared for her.

Sam was glad she had sent Kody home. She knew he wasn't happy about it, but she really didn't want to be around him at that point. She was regretting letting him get too close too fast, and she had only herself to blame. Joe thought the world of him, or so it seemed, but she wasn't going to commit to a relationship that didn't feel one hundred percent right. She knew every relationship had its ups and downs, but lately this one seemed to have more downs than ups. There hadn't been any fights, but she had watched him when they went out and she detected some major jealousy when someone looked at her. She had been hoping she was wrong, but Uncle Chad had always told her "If it feels wrong, it probably is."

"Sam? You okay?" Parker had a concerned look on his face. He was wondering what was going on in her head. He knew it wasn't thoughts of butterflies and roses.
"Huh? Oh, yeah, I'm okay. Sorry...was just thinking."
"About? I know you said you didn't want to talk about anything serious tonight, but the look on your face tells me you're thinking some pretty serious stuff." He took her hand and said, "I'm here if you want to talk Sam. If there's anything you want me to do, anything you want me to say, or anyone's ass you want me to kick - I'm on it."

She squeezed his hand and smiled, "Thanks Parker, but I think I have it under control. I may have to hold you to your word though."

He wondered what she meant by that; he really hoped it wasn't the ass-kicking she was referring to, but he would do it if necessary. He preferred to settle things as calmly as possible, but if it came down to it, he could more than hold his own in a fight.

"I'm going to bed," she said as she got up. "Dad is going to be started on some new meds in the morning and I want to be there. I really hope it helps; he is very ready to come home."

Parker stood up with her, and wrapped his arms around her. God, she smelled good! He loved how her breasts felt against his chest, and the way her hair draped over her bare shoulders. He was very tempted to pick her up and carry her upstairs, but he knew it was not the time. Besides, Simon was sleeping in the spare room and he sometimes didn't have the sense to keep things quiet.

"You had better go to bed Sam." He let go of her and kissed her on the cheek. "Get some sleep. What time do you want me to make coffee?"
"Thanks, I'll try. Make it when you get up; I'll leave my door open so I can smell it. Goodnight Parker."

He watched her as she walked away and took the wine glasses and empty plate to the kitchen. He wished he could have gone with her and given her something else to think about for awhile, but she needed her rest. She was in for some rough days ahead, and she needed to stay healthy. Both for her sake and Joe's.

Parker turned out the lights and laid down on the sofa. He pictured Sam dropping the towel to the floor and standing in front of her mirror, brushing her hair before she crawled into bed. He knew he should just go to sleep, but that image had him throbbing. As he slipped his hand into his boxers he thought about their last night together. He slowly stroked his erection and wished she was there with him. He remembered how good she felt inside, and how she liked him to take her from behind.

As Parker was fantasizing about her, Sam was doing just what he had pictured. She stood naked in front of her mirror and brushed her hair. She thought about him being downstairs, and was pretty sure she could feel the beginning of a hard-on when he hugged her. She had been tempted to press herself against him just a little harder, but knew that would lead to a night of sex. That wasn't a bad thing, but she did have to be up early and had to try to get some sleep.

After she turned out the light she crawled into bed; the first time in days she had been able to sleep nude. She had missed her flannel sheets and the privacy she had at home. She wasn't sure if she could handle sharing her bed with anyone full-time; and if she did, he would have to be willing to give her the space she was used to.

As she laid in the dark, she thought about Parker being downstairs. He hadn't bothered to put on pants when she got home; just stayed in his boxers. She hadn't been surprised by that at all, but sure wished he had covered up a little. She was enjoying the view a little too much, and just by knowing what was under the boxers had her feeling flushed. She had been on her side, but rolled onto her back as she thought about how good Parker felt inside her. She was needing some stress relief, and a little self-pleasure didn't hurt anyone. She gently rubbed her breasts, then slid her right hand down between her legs. She stroked the inside of her thigh, then slipped her finger in between her lips. She was surprised at how wet she was, even with all that had been going on in her head and her life. She teased herself as long as she could stand it, then applied a little more pressure and speed. Her fingers were wet and they slid easily between her lips. She squeezed her breasts and nipples with her left hand and was trying to think of nothing but the pleasure she felt. Other thoughts entered her mind, but she pushed them all away. She only wanted to feel at that moment, not think. She had to stifle her moans as she climaxed, for fear that Parker of Simon would hear her. As she drifted off to sleep, her hands stayed where they had been when she had her orgasm.

Downstairs Parker had been playing his own game, thinking about Sam and picturing her with her legs spread slightly. He had flipped the blanket back, slid his boxers down and put some lube in his hand to reduce some of the friction. It wasn't a good feeling to rub too hard without lubrication; he had caused himself some minor irritation early in his self-pleasuring experience and vowed to not be so hasty. He had gotten to the point in his life where he did what felt good and wasn't afraid to enhance the pleasure; with or without a partner. He knew if it hadn't been for his own hand, he'd be wound so tight sexually that he'd explode the minute a woman touched him. This was his way of keeping things going when he was with someone (and lately that someone had only been Sam months before).

As he stroked and squeezed he could feel the orgasm building. As much as he preferred to do this skin to skin, he slipped on a condom and added more lube. He really didn't want to have to explain any wet spots to Sam (or anyone else for that matter). The condom had reduced a little of the sensitivity he had been feeling, but it didn't take long to reach that point again. As he stroked from base to tip he forced himself to slow down every few strokes. He knew what he liked, and he didn't rush it. Gone were the days of having to rush through a hand job for fear of being caught. The sofa was positioned in such a way that anyone coming into the room couldn't see him as soon as they entered the room anyhow. A quick flip over of the blanket would easily cover him if necessary. Getting up in front of someone on the other hand might pose a problem.

He knew he was taking a little longer than he should, but he was enjoying the sensations. It was late and it was just him and his thoughts. His thoughts continued to be of Sam naked and teasing him with her lips, which kept him hard. Stroke, squeeze, stroke, squeeze. He thought of her lips around his erection, and the little thing she did with her tongue. He increased his speed as he thought of the ease with which she could bring him to orgasm when she wanted to. He also thought of the way she could hold him back as well. There had been times when he had been so close, and she would squeeze the base with her hand and he would lose the feeling he was going to come. He hadn't quite figured out what she did differently than he did; perhaps it was because he couldn't stop himself once he reached a certain point. For her it was easier, because she wasn't stopping herself, she was stopping him. And speaking of not being able to stop himself, he had reached the point of no turning back. He was having difficulty stifling his own moans, just as Sam had. The only bad part now was he couldn't drift off to sleep, as he had to clean himself up.

CHAPTER SEVENTEEN

Sam awoke to the smell of fresh brewed coffee and fried bacon. She looked at the time and hopped out of bed. She had hoped she would have had an earlier start, but it was her own fault for telling Parker the smell of coffee was the only alarm she needed. It had worked, but she wished she had given him an earlier time frame.

As she walked into the kitchen she was pleasantly surprised to see pancakes, bacon, syrup, strawberries and whipped cream on the table, with three plates ready to be filled. Simon poured the coffee and Parker pulled out her chair.

"Why thank you...and good morning you two!"

"Did you get some sleep Sam?" asked Parker.

"Yes, as a matter of fact I did. Much more than I thought I would. What's on your agenda for the day besides chores?"

"I have to leave," said Simon. "I hope that's okay with you?"

"Of course it is Simon. I knew you didn't have many days where you could be here. I do appreciate you taking the time off to help out though. It's a lot of work for one person; especially one who is just learning the ropes." As she made the last comment, she winked at Parker.

"It was nice to get away from the city. I'm glad I could help. I can come out on the weekend again if you need me to."

"We'll keep that in mind Simon. Thank you! Alright, who made breakfast? It's delicious!"

"It was a joint effort," Parker replied.

After breakfast the two men went out to do chores while Sam got ready to go into town. She really hoped the medications would control Joe's seizures so he could be home for awhile. She stopped by the barn on her way and said goodbye to Simon, then told Parker she would see him later that evening. "I expect you to be sleeping in the spare room from now on; of all the places to sleep, you pick the lumpiest sofa."

"It's not that bad," he retorted. He really didn't mind it; it wasn't as bad as she said it was.

When Sam got to the hospital, Jason was already there. He had talked about leaving early, but she still didn't expect him to get there before she did. "Where's Emily? Did she not want to come with you?"

"No, she's having a hard time with all of this. She decided to stay at work and keep herself busy. I think she's torn between Uncle Joe and Sally. I know where my priorities are, but hers aren't the same. Keith is in with him now, finalizing a few documents. The Will has been redone and they are just waiting on the Commissioner of Oaths to get here to witness the changes. Nothing much has changed since you saw it. Sam, about Kody..."

"What about Kody? Did I miss something?" Sam was only asking for clarification, because she had thought it was only her jumping to conclusions that was causing the mixed feelings. He had been acting differently since Joe collapsed, and she couldn't quite figure it out.

"You know he has been helping Uncle Joe here for many years, right?"
"Yeah, but what does that have to do with anything?"
"Uncle Joe has noticed a few things since you arrived on the estate; or should I say, since Kody realized who you were. He has become a little more arrogant, and Uncle Joe is concerned. He has removed Kody as executor as well as relieved him of his 'needing' his help with the farm work. I will be here to help more, and your dad has a

plan for a full-time position which he really hopes Parker can fill. I know this is a lot to take in Sam, but please understand."

"It's okay Jason - I do understand. Kody has been getting to me lately anyhow. I get the feeling he thinks he owns me now that we are a couple, and you know that has never sat well with me. He's nice enough, but the vibes lately are just not what I'm comfortable with. He hasn't talked much about his past relationships, and those he has mentioned it has always been 'her' fault for it not working out. I care for him, but I don't see myself living with him. Jason, I haven't even been invited to stay over at his house. What does that tell you?"

"It tells me a lot Sam. It tells me he does not want to share his world with you, even though you are expected to share yours with him. It tells me he doesn't think you're good enough to show off to his family and friends. And, it tells me he is fully expecting to be given a share of the farm because he has been a regular fixture on it for so many years. I'm just glad enough people have stepped forward to voice their concerns. He has been a member of this community since day one; the residents here know exactly what he's like. Charming and helpful until he gets what he wants, then tosses others aside like yesterday's newspaper."

Sam was floored, but not because Kody had the potential to be an overbearing, jealous boyfriend. She was floored because some members of the community had voiced their concerns to Joe; some even before he collapsed. The members of Bronwin had basically thrown one of their own under the bus to ensure the safety and well-being of an outsider. She still considered herself the outsider, even though they made her feel very welcome indeed. She was still trying to get accustomed to the friendliness of everyone - it was so different in the city.

"Let's go in and see how things are going," said Jason. "He's going to think you forgot about him."
"Good morning Dad! It's Jason's fault I'm late."
"Sure, blame your cousin," Joe replied. "I'm sure he had something to do with it though."
They all laughed; moments like that were few and far between lately.
"Have they given you the new meds yet Dad?"

"Yes, and so far so good. They have talked about a Day Pass for me today, but I haven't got the final okay on it yet. If I do get to go out for awhile, I want to go home."

"Of course you'll get to go home Dad. Where else do you think we'd take you?"

A moment later the Commissioner of Oaths walked into the room and he, Joe and Keith signed the documents they had been working on. Joe felt a sense of relief and the feeling of a weight being lifted from his shoulders. He was glad he had been given a second chance, and that he was able to rectify a mistake he had made before it was too late.

Just before noon, Dr. Green walked in with good news. "Okay Joe, you can leave for a few hours. If anything doesn't feel right, get back here or call the ambulance. If you're not back by 7 I'm sending out a search party."

Joe's face lit up and he said, "Let's blow this popsicle stand!"

The others laughed and Sam helped him get ready. He couldn't wait to get home and out to the barn. He had missed his herd, and wanted to see Lulu; the alpaca responsible for bringing him around.

Jason walked out to the truck with them, then said, "I'm heading back home for a couple days. If you need me back here, just say so. There are some things at work I have to look after."

"Do what you need to do Jay. Sam will take good care of me." He smiled at Sam, then hugged his nephew. "Let us know when you get back to the city."

"Will do Uncle Joe. Sam, call me if you need anything. I don't care what time of day or night it is." Jason hugged Sam and turned away. He didn't want the others to see the tears filling his eyes. Joe hadn't called him Jay since he was a kid; and it was what Chad called him frequently. He missed his dad each and every day; but days like this were almost unbearable without him at his side.

CHAPTER EIGHTEEN

As they pulled into Joe's yard, Parker met them with a smile. "Home for good Mr. Jones, or just for the day?"

"Unfortunately, just for the day," said Joe. "Hopefully soon it will be for good. How is everyone?"

"They are all just fine Mr. Jones. Lulu seems a little disappointed when she sees me walk through the door in the morning, but aside from that she's okay."

"She should be happy to see me then, shouldn't she?" said Joe as he walked toward the barn. Sam had thought about stopping him, then decided not to. If he wanted to go to the barn before the house, then so be it. She was going to do whatever she could to make his remaining time as comfortable and enjoyable for him as possible. She didn't want to see him gone forever and hoped there was something that could be done. She wanted more time with him; years, not weeks.

As Joe walked into the barn he called to Lulu. She heard him and was at the gate in seconds, humming excitedly. She was the only alpaca that would willingly let him catch her, and stand still to be haltered, brushed or even cuddled. The two had a bond that was uncommon, but not unheard of. Joe attributed it to the fact he had bottle fed her when her mother didn't have enough milk for her.

Sam watched him with her, then took a walk up to the loft. She was bound and determined to learn how each and every piece of the equipment worked and what stage of the processing it was used for. She saw the future this room alone held, from the bags of fiber to the weaving loom. She knew Joe didn't have a clue how some of it worked (or so he said), but she was going to find out the name of each piece and research it. She knew some of it had been prototypes her grandfather had made, but she was sure newer models had been built. Some of the plans and rights had been sold to manufacturers, so there had to be some information on it somewhere.

She decided there was no time like the present to start photographing and documenting the equipment. She had been meaning to do it for some time, and now that Joe was home and the court case was over she no longer had any excuses.

While Sam took pictures and made notes on her phone, Joe and Parker talked about the alpacas. Joe quizzed him about the different terms used in the alpaca industry and was surprised that Parker was right each and every time. He had underestimated this young "city slicker". Joe had some advice for Parker as well, and they chatted for quite some time about feed, pasture, shearing and general care of the herd. They also talked about the best type of fencing, gates and breeding pens. "I have this set up so that one person can select and move either one animal or a pen full. It causes less stress for both the person and the animals this way, and there is always an extra gate just in case there is a runaway. When spring rolls around and the grass turns green, I'll show you exactly what I mean."

Parker looked at Joe and said "I don't think I'll still be here when the grass turns green. That's still weeks away, and my holiday time will be coming to an end in a couple of weeks."
"The hell you won't still be here Parker! Who the heck do you think is going to help Sam run this place? I'm not sure how long I'll be able to be out here, and no matter how well I have it set up, she still needs help. It is a lot of work for her to have to do alone."
Parker was confused, and spoke his mind. "I presumed Kody would be helping out, since he has been helping you all these years. Is that not the case? Was I jumping to conclusions?"
Joe laughed, "Damn rights you were jumping to conclusions boy! I have had some time to see the real Kody lately, and it pisses me off that he would take advantage of a dying man that way. I like to give

everyone a fair chance, and he has been a big help out here. I just don't think he's the man for the job, especially since he has his own business in town. I also don't think he's the man for my daughter."

Parker was at a loss for words; had he heard right? Had Joe really just told him he didn't approve of Kody for his daughter?

"And what, Parker, are your intentions with my daughter?"
"Well sir, I adore her to pieces. I'm not sure how much you know, but her and I did date for awhile; even tried living together. We weren't exactly compatible, but have stayed friends. Some people just perhaps shouldn't live together.

"Now that I agree with," said Joe "but with the accommodations available around here, you wouldn't have to see each other if you didn't want to. Now, what do you say? Are you ready, willing and able to learn all I know about these animals?"
"Yes sir, I am."
"Now that's the answer I was hoping for. Shall we go find Sam and tell her the good news?"

CHAPTER NINETEEN

The rest of the day went by smoothly, and Sam drove Joe back to the hospital. Depending on what transpired overnight, he was told he could possibly go home the next day.

Sam was still pretty excited about the decision Joe had made in terms of her 'business partner' and knew she had to break the news to Kody at some point. She was also going to tell him she needed to slow down as far as their relationship went. She wasn't quite sure how well that was going to go over, but it was something that had to be done. Now that she was being given more responsibility on the estate, and had time to re-evaluate her personal situation, she decided perhaps a steady relationship wasn't in her best interest. She had been having second thoughts before Joe collapsed, but the days since had confirmed her misgivings. She was not going to stay in a relationship just because she didn't want to be alone. She didn't mind being alone; and she had her friends and family for when she wanted company.

She decided she would stop by Kody's on the way home and talk to him. She sent Parker a text to let him know, and to call her if she wasn't home in an hour. She also sent him Kody's address, just in case. She wasn't anticipating the visit to go well, and she wanted to have someone watching out for her...just in case.

It was almost 8 when Sam parked in front of Kody's house. As she got out of her truck she was sure she saw another person sitting beside him on the sofa. Perhaps he had company, which was just as well. There was less chance of him causing a scene (or so she hoped) if there was someone else there.

She took a deep breath and knocked on the door, trying to shake the uneasiness she was feeling.

"Sam, what are you doing here?" Kody whispered when opened the door.
"Can we talk for a minute Kody?"
"Now isn't really a good time Sam. You should have called instead of coming here." He stepped out on the front step and closed the door. Sam felt a little more at ease, but couldn't help but wonder why he didn't ask her to come inside.
"I'm sorry, but I thought it was best if I did this in person. I'll get right to the point: with Dad being ill and me having more to do on the estate, I think we should slow down. I really do appreciate all the help you've given us, but things are moving much too fast. I know him being ill isn't easy on you, since you've spent so much time with him over the years. Please understand."
Kody grit his teeth, grabbed her arm and and growled "Are you ditching me for Parker? How convenient!"
"This has nothing to do with Parker! Ow! You're hurting me! Let go of my arm!" Sam was suddenly very afraid. "On second thought, scratch the slowing down. We're done!"
"You bitch! After all I've done for you!"

Just then the door opened. "Who is it Kody?"

Sam took one look at the woman behind him and turned around to leave. As she made her way to her truck she raised her right hand and extended her middle finger.

"Sam! Wait! It's not what it looks like!"

As she drove away from Kody's house, she couldn't believe who had been with him. On second thought, that wasn't entirely true. She could believe it, but it didn't impress her one bit. Once she was around the corner, she stopped her truck and dialed her phone. Jason answered on the first ring. "What's wrong Sam? Is Uncle Joe okay?"

"Dad is back at the hospital, but we have bigger problems at the moment. Emily is with Kody at his house; I think it's in her best interest if you call her and tell her to get out of there. I'm not sure why she's there, but as mad as I am right now, she is family and I think she may be getting in over her head."

"Dammit! I told her to stay away from him!"

"I told him we were done Jason. At first I said we should slow down, but after he grabbed my arm hard I told him we were done. If I have to put up with a temper I'm better off alone."

"Are you okay Sam? I'll deal with Emily. Go home and lock your gate and doors. I'll make a couple of calls."

"Yeah, I'll be fine. Thanks Jason!"

Sam drove home, and locked the main gate behind her. She didn't think it was necessary, but did as Jason had told her. It seemed he knew a little more than she thought he did. She wasn't worried though, because Jason would set Emily straight. She still couldn't help but wonder what Emily had been doing at Kody's. Hadn't Jason said she was working to keep busy?

Parker met her at the door. "I was just about to call you. Is everything okay?"

"Better now that I'm home. Give me a minute; I have to call Jason."

"I'm home," Sam said when Jason answered the phone. "Did you call her? Was she going to leave?"

"I did, and she said she'd handle it. Does she know you called it off?"

"Not unless he told her. She came outside after he called me a bitch."

"Chances are he didn't relay that information, which is probably a good thing. She does her best work when she thinks there's a big risk. She can hold her own Sam; I've seen her take down men twice her size."

"What are you talking about Jason?"

"Let's just say Emily is good at what she does; sometimes she has to cross a line or two to get the information she needs, but it'll be worth it in the end."

Sam was very confused, then it hit her. "Is she a P. I.?"

"Bingo! He doesn't suspect a thing. Now Sam, go get some rest. I trust Parker is still staying with you?"

"Yes, he is. Please fill me in on what the hell is going on soon. I feel like I'm out of the loop."

"I will; just not tonight. Goodnight Sam."

"Goodnight Jason." Sam hung up the phone and turned to see Parker watching her.

"He called you a bitch? Do you want me to set him straight Sam?"

"No Parker, I do not. Apparently Emily has everything under control." Sam shook her head in disbelief, and wondered why Kody was under such scrutiny, and why Emily was the one chosen to get involved. "I just want to go to bed."

Parker was going to say something to the effect of "let's go" but decided now was not the time. He knew the last few days had been rough on Sam, and was not about to be the one to make things worse.

"Do you want a drink Sam? I'll mix you one."

She was about to refuse, then decided it might help her relax a bit. "Yes please. Rum and coke sounds good. I'm going to go take a quick shower, then I'll come down and join you."

He watched her walk toward the stairs, and wished things had been different between them. Maybe there was a reason they didn't click when it came to living together, but he was willing to give it another try. She had been on his mind a lot lately, and now with Kody out of the picture perhaps there was some hope after all. He decided he wasn't going to push the issue though; she didn't go for the controlling boyfriend. He still wanted to go to Kody's and give him a piece of his mind, but figured he wasn't worth the effort.

When he heard the water shut off, he mixed them each a drink. He knew she'd be down in a few minutes, wrapped in only a towel and her hair down. If only she knew how pretty she looked. He lit a candle and set it on the coffee table in the solarium, then went to the linen closet and got a quilt she had made put it on the wicker sofa. It didn't take Mittens long to find the quilt, and he made himself comfy right away. Parker could hear him purring, content as could be. Bear was on the loveseat, taking up the whole thing. Parker couldn't believe how much he had grown in the past couple of months. He was starting to grow into his feet and his coordination was getting better, but he was still a puppy.

Sam walked into the solarium just as Parker knew she would; wrapped in nothing but a towel. She saw the quilt and laughed when she realized Mittens was on it. She sat down beside Parker and tried not to disturb the cat, but her efforts were in vain. Mittens had missed her and crawled onto her lap. Parker took the opportunity to wrap the quilt around her shoulders (but not before noticing some bruising on her upper arm) and handed her the drink.

"Thank you Parker. You know just how to make me feel better."
"Care to tell me about the bruise on your arm? Did Kody get a little rough?"
"Yeah, a little. Made a snide comment about you being convenient when I told him we should slow things down. When he grabbed me that was when I told him to forget slowing down, and that it was over. Emily opened the door right after he called me a bitch."

Parker could feel the anger building, but knew it would do no good to thump on Kody (although the thought made him feel better). He took a deep breath and then took a sip of his drink. It sure tasted good, and he found himself resisting the temptation to down it all at once.

"Do you want to forget the events of the day for awhile Sam? Here, turn around." With that he positioned himself behind her and rubbed her shoulders; moving her hair to one side. He had become quite good at giving massages, and he knew she appreciated them.

They talked about the estate, the things that needed to be done, and the brew that was ready in the conservatory. Sam was feeling overwhelmed with it all, and voiced her concerns.

"It's okay Sam, I'm not going anywhere. We'll work on this together. I'll take the suite above the garage, or I can keep a closer eye on Joe if you want. I'm not going to invade your space; I know how much you enjoy your quiet time."
"It's not just that Parker. I'm terrified of losing him. I am just getting

to know him again; why is this happening to him?"

"That's something I can't answer Sweetie. I wish I could make it all better, but it's out of our hands. Do the best you can and enjoy every minute with him. Don't think about it; just go about your daily routines or start new ones. He's going to need you more, but let him know you need him too. We have a lot to learn about this place; me more than you. Do what you need to and find out all you can about the loft and its contents. I think the best thing we can do is keep him as involved in the day-to-day operations of this place as possible. He'll be much better off, and so will you."

Sam set her empty glass down on the coffee table and leaned against him. He wrapped his arms around her and pulled the quilt over her shoulders once again. He could feel her relax and knew she was falling asleep. He wanted to take her upstairs, but knew it wasn't the right thing to do. She just needed to be held, without any expectations. He decided to walk her upstairs and tuck her in; if they stayed where they were they would both be very sore in the morning. That wicker furniture was great for sitting on, but not so great for sleeping on. She needed a good night's rest; who knew what tomorrow would bring.

"Sam, time for bed. I'll walk you up."

She stood up and sleepily let him lead her up the stairs. He folded back her duvet and she dropped her towel and crawled into bed. He stared at her for a moment, then covered her up. As he leaned over to kiss her forehead she whispered "stay with me". Parker laid down beside her on the bed and pulled the extra quilt up. He wasn't getting under the sheet with her or taking off his clothes; it was too risky. He wasn't going to take advantage of her, even though he wanted nothing more than to make love to her.

CHAPTER TWENTY

Morning found Sam in bed alone, and the smell of coffee gently awoke her. She checked the time and was surprised she had slept several hours. She barely recalled walking up the stairs or Parker laying with her (or perhaps the latter was just a dream). She got out of bed, brushed her hair and got dressed.

"Good morning Sam! Coffee?"
"Would love some. Thanks for helping me upstairs. Sorry I wasn't much fun last night."
"I did what any friend would do. I tucked you in and stayed on my own side of the blankets. How was your sleep?"
"Much better than I thought it would be. Do you want help with the chores before I go into town?"
"No, you go ahead. I'm sure your dad will be chomping at the bit, wanting to leave. I'll take care of things here. Call if Kody shows up at the hospital or gives you any grief. I'll set him straight for you."
"I'm sure all will be fine, but thanks for the offer. I'll keep an eye out for him, but I have a hunch he won't be going anywhere near the hospital."

Sam grabbed a bowl of cereal and finished her coffee, then got ready to leave. "Have you gone into the conservatory lately Parker?"
"Yes, all is well. Your dad's brew is ready too. Maybe he can show me what to do with it today, if he is able to get out on another pass."
"I'm sure he'd love to." Sam looked serious, then said "Are you sure you're ready for all of this Parker? It is a lot of work."

"I am ready Sam. A little hard work never killed anyone. Plus, I'll have the best team player by my side."

Sam blushed a little, then said, "Thanks. I had better get going, or I'll get fired and you'll be doing it all alone."

With that she walked out the door. Parker stood there for a few minutes, thinking about how good she looked. He also thought about what the future held for him. He had never envisioned himself as a "country boy" before, even though Sam told him more than once he was out of place in the city. It seemed she knew him better than he did.

Sam arrived at the hospital and saw Jason's SUV. She wondered if Emily was with him, or if she was with Kody. The previous evening didn't make much sense to her, but lately everything was pretty messed up.

As she walked through the door, she almost ran into Julie. "I'm so sorry Julie! I really must watch where I'm going."

Julie laughed, "It's okay Sam. You have a lot on your mind these days. How are you holding up through all of this?"

"Surviving. It has been pretty crazy the last few days, but maybe it hasn't been a bad thing is some regard. I have been able to see some true colours, and that in itself is a good thing. I don't think those colours would have been revealed otherwise, at least not this quickly."

"Yes, I agree with you there. Joe told me what was going on; I'm glad you were able to see the bigger picture. I have to get to the office, but feel free to stop by anytime. Bring Joe by one day soon; we'll have a good visit."

"Thanks Julie. I would like that, and I'm sure he would too. I had best get to his room or he's going to think I'm not coming today."

"He's in good hands right now. Jason is with him, waiting for you. Have a good day Sam. You know where I am if you want to talk."

After Julie left the building, Sam made her way to Joe's room. Jason was talking as she walked in. "Well, look who decided to show up. We thought you forgot we were here." He winked at her and smiled.

"How did you sleep Sam? Sorry you had to find out the way you did."

"Good morning to you too," she said as she stuck her tongue out at him. "Actually, I slept better than I thought I would, given the conversation I had last night. Has he been here this morning?"

"No, he hasn't. You won't have to worry too much about him; Emily did her part to ensure he'd leave you and Uncle Joe alone. I'm sorry we didn't tell you earlier, but we had to be sure we didn't blow her cover. She's been watching him for some time, and as noble as he seems at first, he is far from it."

"I'm still confused. What has he done to piss off so many people?"

Jason started to speak, but Joe cut him off. "I got this Jay." He looked at Sam and said, "Although he appears to be an upstanding member of the community, he does have a dark side. He is very good at charming the pants off people (no pun intended), only to take what he wants and move on. In your case, he thought he would be able to win you over and take over the financial end of the estate. He forgot he was friends with an ex-cop; and one who liked to do a little investigating of his own. He's not very broken-hearted about this, because he thinks he'll just move on and find some other unsuspecting woman. That's where Emily came in. I told him to watch her because she liked to go for what she couldn't have. He took the bait, and she worked her magic with him. He was well paid for his time he put in on the estate, so don't let him ever tell you it was out of the goodness of his heart.

I needed help, and he was available. Chad knew something was up, but didn't stress out over it. He knew Kody would get found out sooner or later, so he just let it take its course. It's too bad Chad missed out on this, but if it hadn't been for him there would be a lot more people on Kody's side. He can be very convincing, but Chad saw right through it."

"What is it exactly that he goes after?" Sam was still missing something, and she felt stupid for not seeing what they were getting at.

"He's a swindler Sam," said Joe, "and that's putting it lightly. He's also very paranoid. He thinks every woman he goes out with is after his money, but in reality it is the other way around. He gains their trust and then before they know what has happened, he has them signing over ridiculous amounts of money or property. He was a little more careful with you, because he was afraid of getting his ass kicked. It appears he wasn't as careful as he thought, because he will soon be doing time for fraud, embezzlement and assault."

Sam couldn't believe what she was hearing. "Seriously? Do I ever feel like a dumbass! And to think I was falling for him."

"He was executor of my Will, because I didn't have anyone else close by. He thought he would walk with everything when I died, but the joke's on him because I survived. To be honest, it took me a long time to see him for who he really is. I thought he had a small group of haters, but as I started asking questions and doing some detective work of my own, I found out different. It actually worked out with him taking an interest in you Sam; it gave me more time to observe from a distance. I'm sorry you were involved, but as it turns out it worked out. Your Uncle Chad always said things would work out in the end, and he was right."

Jason walked over to Sam. "I'm sorry Sam; I knew what was going on but knew it was best if I stayed on the sidelines. Keith filled me in just before the court case. Up until that point, I was glad you found someone who made you happy. It took me a bit to wrap my head around it too, but we were ready if things would have gone sideways."

"All's well that ends well; isn't that what Uncle Chad used to say to us? Now, what's the plan for today Dad?"

"The plan is I get to go home, but I haven't been cleared by security yet." With that he nodded toward the nurse, and winked at her.

"Mr. Jones, why is it you insist on making me look like such a tyrant?" The nurse scowled at him, then couldn't help but smile.

"If I didn't give you a hard time your days would be uneventful. Now be a dear and let me go home."

"Hold your horses, would you? Maybe I should keep you here today just to protect the rest of society from your shenanigans."

"Fine. Have it your way, but be warned if you keep me here you will not rest today." Joe flashed her an evil smile, and she knew he would pick on her incessantly.

"Let me check with the doctor first. If you're a good boy maybe he'll let you out for a few hours."

She left the room, and could hear Joe laughing. She couldn't help but smile to herself; as rough as he had it, his sense of humour was still strong. She saw too many patients just give up when they were diagnosed with a terminal condition, but not him. She had a feeling he was going to fight it til the end.

A few minutes later she returned to Joe's room with his doctor. "I hear you're harassing my staff...again! Joe, you really need to be nicer to my nurses; they do have free reign with the sharp pointy objects you know. Careful or you might get one or two in your rear end." Dr. Green tried to sound stern, but was failing miserably. "Just to give my nurses some peace and quiet, I'll let you leave for a few hours again today. Curfew is the same as last night, but if something doesn't feel right get yourself back here. I think the medication is working like we want it to, but I don't think I should kick you out completely just yet." He turned to Sam and said, "If you notice anything unusual, get him back here or call the ambulance. I will be available all day, so call me if you have any questions."

"Yeehaw!" Joe was just a little enthusiastic about leaving. Jason and Sam laughed in spite of themselves, and walked on either side of him out to the parking lot.
"Do you mind if I come out to the estate? I hear there may be something ready for me to pick up today."
"Ah, yes. I do believe there is Jason. Parker said it might be ready. Dad, can you help us with your "brew" when we get there?"
"Yes, I'll do what I can. Jason, how much do you have room for? On second thought, get Leon to bring out a truck. We might be able to pump it into a tank and you can bottle it in the city."

Jason made the call to Leon, and gave him directions. Unbeknownst to Jason, Leon knew exactly where to go. He had gone out with Chad on several occasions, but had been sworn to secrecy.

When they got to the estate, Sam parked by Joe's house. He got out and went inside for a few minutes; long enough to change his coat and put on a pair of boots. He then made a trip to the barn, and had a handful of oats ready for Lulu.

"Okay, let's go check on the brew. Where's your business partner Sam?"

"He's already there Dad. He was the one who asked about bottling it today. He is taking his job very seriously."

Well then, let's not keep him waiting. The three of you have a lot to learn; and since that is a by-product of the herd, you all need to know how to mix it. You'll all be cleaning enough of it up." He couldn't help but smile when he thought of them cleaning up the piles. Even though it was the foundation of his brew, he still would rather someone else cleaned it up.

They made their way to the conservatory and spent the next few hours going over the formula for the fertilizer, and Joe showed them where to run the hose to fill the tank on the truck when Leon arrived. Parker and Jason listened and watched, and Sam made notes. She knew she would never remember it all, and knew it was a lot for the others to remember as well. She hoped they wouldn't have to be the ones mixing the concoction with the next barn cleanup, but knew deep in her heart the days with Joe were limited.

The afternoon whizzed by as they talked and laughed. Joe didn't skip a beat, but Sam could see him getting tired. At around four o'clock, she insisted they stop for the day and go to the house and have some supper. She had put a pan of lasagna in the oven an hour earlier when she went to check on Bear. (Most days he went to the conservatory with her, but with the task at hand it was best if he stayed at the house. He wasn't happy about it, and gave Sam the sad puppy dog look when she put him in his kennel.)

After supper Jason and Sam drove Joe back to the hospital, and met with Dr. Green for a few moments. "If all goes well tonight, he will be discharged tomorrow. I'll let you know what Dr. Evans has planned as soon as I find out. He's working on a treatment protocol and should have it ready within the next day or two. He's just waiting on my report."

"He'll be glad to go home. Keep us posted, and thank you so much for helping him."

CHAPTER TWENTY-ONE

Sam was at the hospital bright and early the next morning, wanting to be there when the doctor made his rounds. She realized she was just as anxious for Joe to be discharged as he was. She knew he was getting the best of care, but she preferred to have him home as much as possible.

"Good morning Joe. How do you feel this morning?" Sam had her back to the door when Dr. Green walked in and was startled by the sound of his voice. She realized she was just a little jumpy since she called it quits with Kody.

"Morning Doc. Good enough to go home," said Joe as he flashed Dr. Green his best smile, trying to look as convincing as possible.
"I hear your night wasn't great Joe. I would prefer you stayed another day or two, but seeing as how you have a good support system at home I'm going to let you go. I do insist that someone stay with you around the clock. I'm not saying you can't go about your daily routine, but just take it easy. If something doesn't feel right, get back in here."

Dr. Green turned to Sam. "I'll have his prescriptions at the desk; there are only two for the moment. We'll get his appointments with oncology and radiology booked shortly; my understanding is the treatment can be done at home, provided he doesn't run into any complications."

"Thank you for everything Dr. Green." Sam was on the verge of tears; she suddenly felt very overwhelmed. Perhaps taking some time to talk with Julie wasn't a bad idea after all. The past few days had been a roller coaster, and she knew she had to keep it together for Joe's sake. Plus, there was so much to be done.

A couple of hours after Sam arrived at the hospital, she was walking out the door with Joe at her side. He had been discharged with a prescription and strict instructions to call the ambulance if anything happened. Dr. Green felt it was better than Sam transporting him, especially if he had a seizure. Appointments had been scheduled for the following week with the oncologist and radiology department. They wanted to know exactly what they were dealing with so they knew how aggressive they had to be with treatment.

After a quick stop at the pharmacy, they made their way home. The trip was filled with idle chit-chat as Sam couldn't bring herself to talk about the diagnosis. She didn't want to upset Joe, and feared if she started talking about it she would completely lose it. She made a mental note to call Julie when she got home. Perhaps an invitation to the estate was in order; it would be good for all of them.

"My house or yours Dad?" Sam was getting ready to slow down, but wanted to make sure she knew which driveway she was turning into.
"Mine please Sam. I just want to go home. I need to get out of these clothes; they smell like hospital."
She couldn't help but giggle; she knew she'd do the same thing if it were her. "Okay, I'll drop you off and get you settled. Do you want me to stay?"
"Sam, I'll be fine. I know the doctor's orders, but I just want to have some peace and quiet for a bit. You go home and do what you need to do. I may just have a nap; sleep didn't come easy last night."

She wanted to insist on staying with him, but she knew it would do no good. She had to trust his judgment and told him to be sure he called her if anything happened, or if he felt even the slightest bit off. He reluctantly agreed, and gave her a hug as she was leaving. Sam couldn't help but think about how stubborn he was, and was going to tell him so. It was about then she realized she was very much like him in that regard and decided to keep her mouth shut.

CHAPTER TWENTY-TWO

Sam suddenly felt mentally exhausted. The events of the past few days were beginning to take their toll on her, and she knew it wouldn't help Joe if she couldn't function. She dialed Julie's number, fully expecting to get the answering machine.

"Hello? Julie speaking. How may I help you?"
"Julie? It's Sam. I was expecting your machine to pick up. Can I take you up on that offer you made at the hospital the other morning?"
"Of course Sam. Would you prefer I made a house call? That way I can talk to Joe too, if that's okay?"
"A house call would be great Julie. Thank you! I was hoping you could fit me in this afternoon. Are you busy?"
"I took the afternoon off. I went to the hospital to see Joe and they told me he went home. I can be there in an hour. Where would you like me to go? Your house or his?"
"Please come to mine. He said he was going to have a nap, and I would like to talk to you alone."
"That works Sam. I'll be there in an hour."

After Sam hung up the phone she went to the kitchen to make some tea. It wasn't even noon yet, and it felt as if she had been up for hours. A cup of peppermint tea would be just the thing to wake her up a bit. As she reached into the cupboard for a cup, she noticed a note on the counter. "Lunch is in the fridge; enjoy."

Sam opened the fridge to find a plate with egg salad sandwiches and carrot sticks. Parker had thought of everything once again. She couldn't help but smile, then sent him a text. "Thanks for lunch. :)" She hadn't planned on eating, but considering he had thought of her she sat down at the table with her tea, the plate and the notepad app open on her phone.

She hadn't forgotten about holding a Writer's Retreat in the Conservatory. She hadn't mentioned her thoughts to Joe yet, as all hell had broken loose before she had the chance. She figured it would be a good thing to discuss with him later in the day; it would help take their minds off the diagnosis. She made some notes and ate her lunch. She wondered what Parker was up to, but didn't want to appear like she was checking up on him. Instead she used the few minutes before Julie's arrival to water the plants in the solarium.

Shortly before one Julie drove into the yard, right on time.

Sam opened the door when she heard the knock. "Thank you so much for coming. Please come in. Can I get you anything? Coffee? Tea?"
"Tea please Sam. And you're very welcome. I needed to get out of town anyway. It's nice to do house calls once in awhile. Days like today shouldn't be spent inside anyway."
"With that being said, would you like to take a walk to the Conservatory? Then we can go over and see how Dad is feeling after his nap."
"That sounds like a great idea Sam. I would love to take a walk through the place."

Sam grabbed a couple of travel mugs from the cupboard, made their tea and they headed out the door, with Bear running ahead down the path. They talked on the way about Joe and his upcoming treatment. Sam felt no reservations about confiding in Julie, considering she was going to be personally affected as well. It had been a long time since her and Sam talked, and things had changed drastically since then.

They walked along the paths in the Conservatory (Bear had taken up his usual spot by the entrance) and talked about recent events with Kody, Sam's new business partner, the future of the estate and the

119

equipment in the loft. Sam voiced her concerns about being able to run the estate without Joe there by her side, and that was when the tears came. Up until that point she had been doing okay, but saying it out loud was too much. Julie led her to one of the many benches, and they sat down. Julie let Sam cry; she said it was healthier to cry than to keep it all inside. She could feel her own tears welling up, but knew it was best if she saved her own crying until later. If Sam was anything like Joe, she'd feel bad for upsetting her. Julie was there to help Sam, not the other way around. She had her own counselor she could confide in; even therapists needed therapy occasionally.

After about ten minutes, Sam composed herself and told Julie about her thoughts on the Writing Retreat. "That's a wonderful idea! This is the perfect setting. Just let me know when you're planning it and I'll help any way I can."

"I haven't said anything to Dad yet; that is this afternoon's project. I have some ideas written down, which I hope he agrees with."

"I'm sure he'll be on board one hundred percent. He is very proud of you Sam. He knows how hard you have worked to get where you are. This place will allow you to realize your full potential. It has everything you need; an uncovered dream if you will. From what your dad says, you are willing to make it all work. Don't give up your writing to take care of everything else; that's where your business partner and dad come in. I understand your cousins are willing to help you out as much as they can as well; let them."

Sam thought for a minute. "I have been thinking about fiction lately. I have written on numerous topics over the years; now I would like to try my hand at a novel. I have a few hundred words written already, but haven't done anything with it since before the court date."

"My advice to you Sam: don't stop writing now. Make the time; those around you will understand. Stop trying to be super woman and take some time for you; if it means locking you in here for a few hours a day, then so be it. I'm pretty sure your dad will agree with me on this one. Now. speaking of your dad, shall we go see him?"

Joe had just woken up when he heard the knock, then footsteps in his house.

"Dad?" called Sam. "Are you in here?"

"Right here," he said sleepily. "I just woke up. I can't believe I slept for two hours."

"How do you feel Dad?"

"Better after a nap in my own bed, with no nurse poking and prodding me at all hours." It took Joe a few seconds to realize Sam had someone with her. "Hi Julie! I didn't see you there. To what do I owe the pleasure?"

Julie gave him a kiss on the cheek. "I just wanted to make sure you were listening to the doctor's orders. I see so far you are behaving."

"I'll do whatever it takes to stick around awhile longer. I intend to fight this to the bitter end."

Sam saw the worry cross his face. She couldn't imagine what he was feeling, knowing his time was limited. She decided to change the conversation and give him something else to think about. "Dad, I've been tossing an idea around in my head for a little and would love to hear your thoughts on it. Do you want me to make some tea and then we can do some brainstorming?"

"Uh oh," Joe teased. "Brainstorming sounds like a make-work project."

The three of them laughed, and Julie and Joe sat side by side on the sofa while Sam made tea and found some cookies to go with it. She set the tray of cups, teapot and cookies on the coffee table, then got to the point.

"I have an idea for a use for the bunker. Since it is all equipped with beds, a functional kitchen and a beautiful conservatory above it, I was thinking of holding a Writer's Retreat. It would be the perfect place for writers to gather and do what they do best. What do you think?"

"I think you should do what you think is best Sam. If you think you can utilize the bunker for something like that, then by all means, do it. It just sits there unused for the most part. If you want to open up the Conservatory to the public as well you can do that too. Perhaps that is something you and your partner should discuss. I'll help you with whatever I can, but the final decisions will be up to you. I trust you'll be able to enlist the help of your friends, or hire some part time help?"

"I'm sure we can work something out." Sam was grinning ear to ear, and spent the next few minutes running some thoughts by Joe. As they sat there drinking their tea, eating cookies and working out a few details in terms of the Conservatory tours, she wished the moment would never end. It felt so good to just talk about the plants, her plans and push the past few days' events out of her mind.

"Sam, no matter what you decide, don't forget to involve Parker. He'll most likely tell you to go ahead and do what you want, but keep him involved. He seems like the type of guy that will follow you to the end of the Earth; work with him as much as you can. I think he's going to do just fine out here, but he's going to need a little guidance and educating - especially where the farming is concerned. He has stepped up to the plate, and I see a lot of potential in him. I just can't believe he has spent all this time in the city, when he clearly belongs in the country."

"That's what I kept telling him Dad. He might believe it now that someone else is on my side. He has yet to agree with me one hundred percent."

"I can clearly see he is enjoying himself out here. Speaking of which, shall we go find him? I want to get you two familiar with some of the equipment in the loft. Julie, care to tag along?"

Julie looked at Joe affectionately, and said "Don't mind if I do".

CHAPTER TWENTY-THREE

Joe spent the days between his release from the hospital and his appointments with the oncology and radiology departments teaching Sam and Parker as much as he possibly could. The days went by quickly, and he kept himself busy. The nights were a different story, as that was when he thought too much. He worried about Sam most of all. He sincerely hoped the treatment he was about to undergo would work to eliminate the tumour in his brain. He wasn't ready to die yet; he still had some fight left in him.

Sam awoke the day of Joe's appointments relieved to see the sun. She had dreaded the thought of the weather turning bad; she preferred not to have to drive in miserable weather if she could help it.

Once again, Parker had the coffee made and breakfast almost ready. He was an early riser by nature, and having something to do before the sun came up seemed to make his days go better. He knew Sam was not very functional that early in the day, so he did what he could to make her morning go smoother.

As she walked into the kitchen, she smiled and said, "You're spoiling me Parker. I could get used to this."
"You have a long day ahead of you. I'd hate to send you on your way without a coffee and food in your belly."

"My nerves and belly thank you for it." She sat at the table and Parker poured her a coffee. He then set a plate with bacon, eggs and toast in front of her. "If this doesn't get you moving, nothing will."

Sam giggled and the two of them ate breakfast together. They talked about the day ahead, and what the game plan was. She was well aware of the fact she might be spending a few days in the city with Joe, which of course depended on the outcome of the scans and appointment with the oncologist. She had packed a small suitcase, just in case. She wanted to be prepared this time.

After breakfast she helped Parker clean up, then said her goodbyes to Bear and Mittens. As she walked out the door, she kissed Parker on the cheek. "Thank you for all your help. I'll let you know when we get there, and what we learn."

He watched her get into her truck and head down the drive. He wished he could have gone along, but he knew his place was now on the estate. If she needed him, she would let him know. That was one thing he adored about her; there was no beating around the bush. She was very much in tune with what she wanted and/or needed, and if she needed him she'd tell him so (not necessarily with words).

The drive to the city was uneventful, and Sam and Joe spent the majority of the time talking about the upcoming work that needed to be done in the barns and Conservatory. Neither of them could bring themselves to talk about the impending appointments, for fear of breaking down in tears.

Sam parked her truck and the two of them made their way to the radiology department. Sam was very afraid of what the outcome would be; afraid the tumour had increased in size. She was not ready for any of this, but ready or not it was something she had to deal with.

As they waited for Joe to be called in for his CT scan, Sam couldn't help but notice how little some of the patients were. One was just a baby that didn't look more than a few days old. She prayed it wasn't cancer that had the little one there, but it was becoming so common in all ages.

The waiting room was busy, and people came and went. The waiting room was shared by both the CT technicians and x-ray technicians, so they were anticipating a bit of a wait. There was also priority given to emergency cases, but so far it didn't appear there was anyone being rushed in. Sam hoped it wouldn't happen, but completely understood if it did.

Fifteen minutes after Joe's scheduled appointment time, he was called in. Sam stood to go with him, but Joe said, "It's okay Sam. I think I can handle this on my own." He gave her a hug and followed the nurse down the hall.

She watched him walk away, feeling a sense of dread. She wondered how much time they really had together. So much had happened in the last few months and she suddenly felt very overwhelmed. Talking to Julie had helped considerably; without her insight Sam knew she'd be a basket case. It was at that point she decided she was going to start a journal and make note of appointments, treatment and all other aspects that went with Joe's illness and remaining days. It would help them keep on track, as well as provide her with information she may need in the future.

Joe emerged about half an hour after he went in. Sam wanted to ask him how it went, but she knew the technician wouldn't have said anything. All they had to do now was wait for the appointment with Dr. Evans.

"Let's grab a bite to eat Sam. Starving ourselves isn't going to help anything."

She checked the time and saw they still had just over an hour before his appointment. "Let's go across the street to the Timmy's; it'll be better than anything here."
"Now that sounds like a plan." Joe's eyes got brighter with the mention of Timmy's. He had a weak spot for the cappuccinos and Boston Cream doughnuts.

Less than an hour later they were in the waiting room of the oncology department. Neither had said much since they made their way back into the hospital as both were lost in thought.

When Joe was called into the examining room, Sam stood to go with him once again. This time he didn't refuse; he wanted her to hear what the doctor had to say. Besides, it would be better if she was there so they had a better chance of remembering all they were going to hear.

"Good afternoon Joe," said Dr. Evans, "I am going to get right to the point, as we have a lot to cover. Please, sit down."

Joe and Sam sat beside each other, and facing the doctor. He had an image on the screen of his computer, and turned the monitor so they could see it. "This is what your head looks like on the inside Joe. See this dark mass here?" With that he pointed to a dark spot about the size of a silver dollar. "It is larger than when the last scan that was done. It is increasing in size quickly, and it appears to be sending out tendrils. That is not a good thing. We have to start treatment immediately if you want any chance of beating this. Even then, there are no guarantees."

"Can I have a day or two? I want to get my affairs in order before I start any aggressive treatment, just in case." Joe's voice cracked as he spoke, and Sam was having a very hard time keeping it together.

"No more than 48 hours Joe. At the rate this is growing, your window isn't very big. I would rather admit you right now and start treatment first thing in the morning, but I can't force you to do that. Do what you need to do, then get back here and let us do what we can to at least slow it down."

"What is the treatment protocol?" Sam was wondering what they were faced with, and made some notes as the doctor spoke.

"Here is a book on this type of cancer. Take it home, read it and make your decisions. There isn't a pleasant way to do any of this. I would love to sugarcoat it, but that doesn't help anyone. All it does is piss people off when they find out the seriousness of the situation."

A NEW NORMAL

CHAPTER ONE

As they left the doctor's office they had tears in their eyes. The prognosis was not good; not good at all.

Sam drove to Jason's house; she had called him from the hospital and asked him to meet them there. Emily met them there as well, as she was going to be a part of the care-giving team. It wasn't going to be easy, but they had to do all they could to keep it together for as long as they had to.

Sam felt so helpless; there was nothing she could do to make it all go away. The treatments would have to start as soon as possible. The doctor was going to admit Joe that very day, but he asked for a couple days to get his affairs in order. He wasn't expecting to get through this one, so wanted to be ready.

As they walked into Jason's house, the tears started to flow.

OTHER WORKS BY DIANE ZIOMEK

FICTION
The Hidden Estate

NONFICTION
Success...It Starts With You!
The Homemaker Helper Series:
Crafts
Writeful Advice
Alpaca to Afghan (in progress)

<<<<>>>>